Hana's Secret

Hana's Secret

A Jack Davidson Medical Mystery

Book One

Jack Langley, M.D.

iUniverse, Inc.
New York Lincoln Shanghai

Hana's Secret
A Jack Davidson Medical Mystery

Copyright © 2007 by Jack Langley, M.D.

All rights reserved. No part of this book may be used or reproduced by any means, graphic, electronic, or mechanical, including photocopying, recording, taping or by any information storage retrieval system without the written permission of the publisher except in the case of brief quotations embodied in critical articles and reviews.

iUniverse books may be ordered through booksellers or by contacting:

iUniverse
2021 Pine Lake Road, Suite 100
Lincoln, NE 68512
www.iuniverse.com
1-800-Authors (1-800-288-4677)

This is a work of fiction. All of the characters, names, incidents, places, organizations, and dialogue in this novel are either the products of the author's imagination or are used fictitiously.

ISBN-13: 978-0-595-42371-2 (pbk)
ISBN-13: 978-0-595-86707-3 (ebk)
ISBN-10: 0-595-42371-X (pbk)
ISBN-10: 0-595-86707-3 (ebk)

Printed in the United States of America

Prologue

▼

Evansville, N.C.—December 7, 2005

If God himself had been standing on the front steps of the York County Courthouse in downtown Evansville that cold Wednesday morning in December, and had personally made the startling announcement that greeted its citizens as they awoke, it could not have been received with more disbelief than had occurred. They were aghast at the news that the administrator of their highly revered Midsouth Regional Medical Center (Midsouth) had been arrested at the regional airport while attempting to flee the country to South America.

Equally incredulous was the additional news that numerous prominent physicians associated with that same institution, several of their wives, and various hospital personnel had also been taken into custody in an early morning sting operation. Initial reports were sketchy and did not indicate the circumstances that had prompted this seemingly incongruous action.

The reports did indicate that the action had followed a lengthy investigation by local police working in conjunction with state and federal authorities. It was not immediately clear what necessitated the involvement of the F.B.I.

Even more shocking was the news of the arrest of Dr. Russell Callahan, Chief of Radiology at Midsouth, accused of the attempted murder of Dr. Jack Davidson, prominent local general surgeon. Dr. Davidson, an inpatient at Midsouth, was recovering from near fatal injuries sustained in a motor vehicle accident several weeks earlier when the murder attempt occurred.

And meanwhile, in his cell at the York County jail, Bill contemplated his fate and thought back to the beginning...

CHAPTER 1

▼

Midsouth—October 24, 2005

It had begun as a routine afternoon in the Radiology Department at Midsouth. Dr. Kevin Bledsoe had scheduled an ERCP for one p.m. The patient had been premedicated and placed on the x-ray table in the special procedure room. The fluoroscope had been checked and positioned. All was in readiness for his arrival.

Kevin entered the room and signaled for the anesthetist to proceed with the I.V. medications as he donned his x-ray apron. The patient was instantly rendered unconscious. The anesthetist signaled for Kevin to begin the procedure.

He carefully inserted the special side-viewing endoscope into the patient's esophagus; proceeding, he skillfully guided it through the stomach and into the patient's duodenum where it came to rest opposite the opening of the common bile duct: the ampulla or papilla of Vater.

Next he guided a tiny catheter through the small opening into the bile duct and began injecting dye.

At this point in the procedure, X-ray films would ordinarily be taken to demonstrate the presence or absence of foreign objects such as gallstones or tumors. Stones, if present, could be removed with special balloon catheters or small basket devices. A tumor could be biopsied, or possibly even removed.

And as a final maneuver, the muscular sphincter of Oddi, the last part of the bile duct, could be incised with a special cutting instrument, allowing the passage of small retained fragments of stone, should any inadvertently remain, a procedure referred to as *sphincterotomy.*

On this particular day, Kevin was performing the procedure on a *project* patient. Russ Callahan was the radiologist in charge and responsible for everything going well.

He had personally interpreted the ultrasound exam several days earlier and certified that the patient had gallstones and an enlarged common bile duct. After conversing with Kevin, they had mutually concluded that she met all the criteria for a *project* patient and needed a diagnostic ERCP.

Their team had seen to it that appropriate lab results were included in her chart. They had prepared the usual special concoction for injection into the common bile duct at the proper point in the procedure.

The team had performed the procedure dozens of times without incident, so there was no reason to anticipate anything different this day in an otherwise healthy patient.

Pictures from the final injection sequence were taken and Kevin put out his hand to receive the specially prepared syringe from Russ. Without fanfare, he injected the contents through the catheter into the common duct as if it were a routine part of the procedure.

No one appeared to notice the minor aberration in his technique.

Several minutes passed as final pictures were taken.

Suddenly, the anesthetist threw back the drapes covering the patient, startling everyone, especially Kevin and Russ.

"What the hell?" were the first words out of Kevin's mouth ... words that were drowned out by shouts of "Call a Code Blue" by the anesthetist. The patient had suddenly become apneic ... unable to breathe ... and pulseless.

Shouts of "Code Blue" reverberated throughout the Radiology Department. People poured into the room from every portal. Emergency department personnel wheeled in carts bearing an array of life saving medications, breathing apparatus and cardiac defibrillators and pacemakers. Bells continued to sound and the overhead intercom blared out intermittently:

"Code Blue: Radiology Department."

Kevin and Russ stared at each other. They stood silent as the emergency department physician, now present, assumed the lead in the resuscitation effort. They could do little but stand and observe, and wonder why this was happening now, how it would impact the *project* and how it would ultimately end.

Chapter 2

▼

Midsouth—July 2005

Midsouth Regional Medical Center (Midsouth) is a 350+ bed acute care hospital complex sprawling over seventy-five acres of prime land in the heart of Evansville, North Carolina, the states fourth largest metropolitan area. In medical parlance, the hospital has all of its beds actively used for varying kinds of medical and surgical problems, with none allocated for nursing home patients ... a ploy used by many smaller hospitals to enhance the apparent size and prestige of their facility.

Midsouth had its own Extended Care Facility (ECF), and Rehabilitation Center. These two facilities, together with the main hospital, made the bed total for the Midsouth campus approach five hundred.

William D. (Bill) Smithson, M.D., President and CEO of Midsouth Regional Medical Center, stood at the entrance to the campus and marveled at the size and complexity of it all. He tried in his mind's eye to picture how it had looked when he first joined the administrative staff there some twenty-five years earlier when it had been just plain Midsouth Hospital.

He had moved to Evansville after completing a Master's degree in hospital administration at the University of Alabama's Birmingham campus, a year of preparation that had served to launch his career well. At about the midpoint of his tenure, when he had already risen to the level of senior associate administrator, the institution had sponsored his return to school to obtain a medical doctor degree.

The institution's ultimate goal was for Bill to become the administrator of Midsouth. The increasing complexity of the relationship between medical practitioners and hospital administrations dictated the need for an individual so trained to sit at the helm of this large and increasingly complex institution.

Shortly after Bill's return to Evansville, the title of President and CEO of Midsouth was suddenly thrust upon him with the untimely death of his predecessor, John Belk.

The original Midsouth Hospital had an inauspicious beginning as a part of the Hill-Burton Act, a federal government program begun in the 1940's that sponsored healthcare facility construction and renovation in the post-WWII era to underserved communities, provided that the facility allocate a percentage of its care to citizens without health insurance free of charge or at reduced rates. Many hospitals built under the program had long since been razed and replaced with modern facilities.

But not Midsouth Hospital!

It had survived to become the core of the medical center complex. The original building had been constructed on land donated by one of Evansville's founding families and now housed a collection of Evansville and York County memorabilia. It had been preserved for posterity, and remained the keystone upon which other buildings had been erected piecemeal over the ensuing decades.

Surveying his small empire, Bill could scarcely discern the original structure, now engulfed by the additional clinical, research and office facilities. Their ***Comprehensive Cancer Center*** with full time specialists in medical, surgical and radiation oncology remained a model in a state replete with several of the best known medical school complexes in the country.

At age fifty-six, Bill was at the zenith of his career. He commanded a workforce of over a thousand employees with an annual institutional budget extending into the tens of millions of dollars, making him a major force among Evansville's business leaders, and in the various healthcare alliances to which Midsouth subscribed. Bill had already served two one-year terms as chairman of the tri-state health group, comprised of representatives from fifty-three facilities in North Carolina and its neighbors, South Carolina and Virginia.

"Regional Medical Center" he thought, as he gazed out over the campus.

"We've come a long way from just plain old 'hospital'." The latter term had become obsolete with the addition of the outpatient surgical facility, the Cancer Center, Rehabilitation Hospital, Children's Hospital and ECF.

And just as the colleges of old had melded into the universities of today, hospitals had transitioned into complex medical centers.

And Bill Smithson had been the major facilitator of that transition in Evansville. As a trained physician, as well as hospital administrator, Bill had a unique perspective with which to conduct his business. He was able to relate well with the medical staff (of which he was a non-practicing member), and the Board of Directors, comprised mostly of business leaders like himself.

Bill had lost his first wife to breast cancer just before returning to school to obtain his medical education. Together, they had three children, all of whom were now grown.

Bill's current wife, Margaret … or Maggie as she preferred to be called … had met Bill while he was completing his medical studies. Her late husband, a family practitioner, had died in an auto accident several years earlier. He had had three daughters from a former marriage; Maggie had helped raise them only briefly. The girls had long since gone their separate ways and remained estranged from her.

So Maggie, at Bill's side for almost five years, had witnessed some of the growth of Midsouth and Evansville. No longer a sleepy southern town, Evansville was as life giving to the region as the life sustaining medical institution that sat in its midst.

Maggie Smithson spent the bulk of her days performing various collateral duties as wife of the CEO of Midsouth. Volunteer services played a large part in fulfilling the needs of the budding giant that was the medical center. In an effort to contain costs, hospitals had come to rely heavily on the aid provided by community minded citizens and charitable service organizations … at no cost to the hospital except for an occasional awards dinner. And Maggie, who had been instrumental in organizing these volunteer groups, now held the title of Chief of Volunteer Services.

Her duties called for almost constant exposure to the public. She maintained a fierce daily fitness schedule that called for early morning jogging, an afternoon workout at the YMCA, and constant vigilance in her eating habits.

At age fifty-five, just a year younger than her husband, she maintained a size ten figure, naturally brunette hair with only a whisper of gray, and a complexion the envy of women ten years her junior.

"Genes" she would say when asked the secret of her youthful looks. She preferred not to reveal the effort she expended in preserving those looks.

Bill, in stark contrast, did little more than his hectic daily schedule required him to do; yet he was able to maintain a trim and youthful appearance. At six foot one, he carried his one hundred and ninety pounds well. His hair had remained jet black except for some distinguishing graying of the temples and faint balding of the crown of his head.

Bill's three children all lived apart from home. The oldest, Bill, Jr., now twenty-eight, had completed law school three years earlier, and was now a junior partner in a large law firm in Raleigh, where he was the firms specialist in medical malpractice law.

Bill, Jr., had married the summer following his graduation from law school. He and his wife Carole were now expecting their first child ... and the first Smithson grandchild.

Susan, the middle child and only girl, was twenty-five. A Merit Scholar, she had graduated from Harvard with honors, earned a Master's degree at the same institution, and was now in the final stages of earning a doctorate degree in international studies. She was currently negotiating a teaching position on the faculty of Georgetown University in Washington, D.C., where her specialty area would be the former soviet bloc countries. She spoke Russian fluently.

Robert, the youngest of the Smithson children, was now twenty. He was a senior at N.C. State, majoring in business administration with plans to follow in his father's footsteps in the healthcare industry after earning a master's degree in hospital administration.

* * * *

Bill's day was already hectic. He had tired of the constant interruptions by his secretary with the intercom beeping incessantly. When he was just on the verge of telling her to hold all calls, she announced that Sarah Coleman was on the line. Sarah, the wife of one of the staff surgeons, Dave Fortner, was due to retire from the now part-time position as soon as a suitable replacement was found ... which couldn't be soon enough for Bill.

Sarah was Vice President of Patient Care, a position formerly called Director of Nursing. Her request was straightforward ... for a change. But the mere mention of her name still caused beads of sweat to form on Bill's brow, his blood pressure to soar at the sound of her voice, and his pulse to race at the very thought of her.

But mostly, it caused his stomach to burn.

"Hi, Bill", came the soft voice from the other end of the phone.

"I need to ask a small favor of you. We're planning a reception for some potential nurse recruits next Wednesday and would love to have you say a few words to them. You know how important you are to the institution, and I know that they would love to hear from the man who has shaped it the most."

Bill knew that there was no refusing her anything, even if this was business. He damned the subtleness of her ways under his breath.

"Sarah, let me check with Martha to see what my schedule is like on Wednesday." He put her on hold while he instructed his secretary to accommodate the request ... no matter what needed to be rearranged.

"Martha will arrange it for you, Sarah. I'll look forward to seeing you and talking to your potential new nurses."

As he hung up the phone, he could feel his body muscles stiffen. Mostly he could feel his stomach on fire. As he reached into his desk drawer for the bottle of antacid tablets he kept in reserve, he breathed a sigh of relief that the request had been simple this time.

CHAPTER 3

▼

Evansville, N.C.—July 2005

Jack Davidson was the current Chief of Surgery at Midsouth, a position that placed an extra burden on his otherwise already busy schedule. Meetings scheduled at various times during the morning, noontime and early evening were becoming all too frequent for the chiefs of services. Weekend retreats, often held out of town, compounded the free time consumption problem. While Lynn, Jack's wife, understood the reason for his frequent absence from home, she didn't have to like it.

She knew that as her husband's stature in the community had grown, so too had his responsibilities. When they were first married ... and young, they thought that advancing age and seniority in the profession would bring a slowdown of such obligations. But in fact, the reverse had been true.

Twenty years of marriage had produced three wonderful children. The oldest was in college and the two youngest were in high school. The couple was anticipating the graduation of the younger two so that they would be emancipated from some of their parental duties. Hopefully, they would then have more time for activities that had been so often postponed, especially traveling.

* * * *

Jack had a busy surgical schedule followed by office hours from one to five p.m. And stuck in the middle of the day was a luncheon meeting of the surgical review committee that he would chair. The agenda called for the usual case reviews and routine items that could be dispatched quickly.

Following the formal meeting that was brief as anticipated, he was approached by several department members who expressed concerns about one of their colleagues, Dave Fortner.

"Jack". Stan Harris spoke for the small group remaining after the general meeting.

"We're concerned about Dave Fortner. The nurses and O.R. techs continue to talk about his speed on gallbladder cases. Frankly, it frightens them because they're afraid he's not paying attention to the anatomy as much as he's concentrating on beating his own record for time. He's down to fifteen minutes with some cases.

And, the rumors continue to circulate about numerous gallbladders that don't have any stones present when checked in the O.R. before being sent to pathology. And there's the issue about perhaps too frequent pre-op ERCP's being done.

We'd like you to investigate and let us know what you find."

For the past fifteen years, Jack and his general surgery colleagues had been performing laparoscopic procedures, principally for removal of the gallbladder. Dave Fortner had been an early proponent of the procedure and had virtually cornered the market at Midsouth, performing almost seventy-five percent of all those done there. The remaining twenty-five percent of cases had to be shared among a dozen or so other surgeons.

Jack had to assume that these complaints, at least those emanating from other surgeons, most likely represented the outcries of jealous colleagues looking for some way to cash in on the goldmine that Dave Fortner controlled. Times were changing rapidly in surgery, and everyone wanted a piece of the hottest action and its attendant cash rewards. And right now, surgical laparoscopy was hot.

ERCP or endoscopic retrograde cholangiopancreatography was no longer a new procedure in gallbladder disease diagnosis, but was one that belonged to the specialty of gastroenterology and was still finding its proper place in the overall evaluation process. Jack had to consider that Kevin Bledsoe, who performed most of the procedures for Dave Fortner, might be performing the right procedure for the right indication and just be a little ahead of his time as Dave Fortner had been.

These matters would require even more of Jack's time and would require tact and diplomacy in obtaining the necessary information upon which to form an opinion. The missing stone issue would require input from Mike Herman, the pathology representative on the surgical review committee, and Russ Callahan from Radiology. Jack had never heard such an allegation raised before at Midsouth or anywhere else.

Frankly, he thought the whole thing was just going to be a waste of his time.

"Dave is a good general surgeon. It's probable that with the high volume of gallbladder cases that he does, he's just gotten better at it than the rest of us.

I've never heard of any Quality Assurance issues concerning him around the hospital. And why would he want to falsify results? I think it's all petty jealousy," he thought to himself.

"I'll make some inquiries and get back to you when I can", he said to Stan and the others.

And now he was late for the office.

*   *   *   *

John "Jack" Davidson was fifty-eight years old and had practiced surgery at Midsouth for almost twenty-five years. He had grown up in Rockland County, which abutted York County on its southwest side. After completing high school, he accepted a scholarship to Northwestern University in Evanston, Illinois. Having been a standout on the debate team, he had chosen Northwestern because of their strong forensics program. The school had expressed a strong interest in him, having seen his work during the national high school competition in which Jack's team had won first place.

His excellent grades throughout his four years at Northwestern, coupled with his affable personality and good looks, and an extremely well rounded extracurricular activity roster assured him the postgraduate training program of his choice.

Jack's choice was medicine. He hoped to follow in the footsteps of his grandfather who had been an old time country doctor in (then) rural York County, before Midsouth Hospital had opened its doors, when doctors still made house calls using a horse and buggy.

His intent was to carry on both the family name and profession. His grandfather had willed him his original doctor's bag and several of his old instruments that Jack now proudly displayed in his office.

Jack graduated from Washington University medical school in St. Louis and then completed surgical residency at the affiliated Barnes Hospital. While he briefly considered family practice, after completion of his clinical rotations while in medical school, he had chosen surgery because it afforded him the ability to make a diagnosis and then confirm it with a surgical procedure when indicated.

Jack had met his future wife, Lynn, during his final year at Barnes. An R.N., she worked in the surgical I.C.U. They married at the completion of his residency training. Following a one-year fellowship in vascular surgery, also at Barnes, Jack joined the United States Navy and was assigned to the Naval Hospital, San Diego, California for his full three-year tour. Following the grueling year of fellowship, it was like an extended honeymoon.

In addition to the luxury of living in southern California for three years at government expense, Jack and Lynn were able to take several space available flights to Hawaii and the Far East and spend a three-week temporary duty assignment at the Naval Hospital, Naples, Italy.

The three years had passed quickly and the time rapidly approached to choose a practice site. Lynn hailed from Wisconsin, and both she and Jack agreed that winters there were much too harsh. They had had enough of those during their time in St. Louis,

The natural choice was to return to somewhere close to Jack's home in the sunny south. When they heard of Midsouth's need for surgeons in Evansville, they were quickly sold. The timing couldn't have been more perfect. They arrived at Midsouth at about the same time that Bill Smithson had signed on as an assistant administrator.

* * * *

The office had been long, but things had gone smoothly. Jack made a quick stop by the hospital to check on a post-op patient and then headed home. It had been a typically long day.

It was great to get home at a respectable hour … which he defined as anything before eight p.m. He and Lynn were beginning to savor such moments more as they grew older.

"I fixed one of your favorites," she said, as he came into the kitchen and gave her a kiss.

"Mmm. Smells good all the way from the front door. Must be your special pork chops."

"I know how you like them."

When they were first married, Jack thought her recipe calling for cooking fatty pork chops in condensed milk and topped with sugar sounded like a sure recipe for a heart attack; not to mention … he just didn't find it appealing. But it had come to be one of his favorites … along with her homemade mashed potatoes topped with real butter.

After they finished dinner, Jack got the coffee and the couple adjourned to their screened-in porch. With the children out for the evening, it afforded them an opportunity to discuss personal matters. Though Lynn had not worked in Jack's office for years, she relied on the office manager, Debbie, to keep her abreast of office activity.

"Debbie tells me that office receipts have slipped almost ten percent from this time last year. You certainly don't seem to be working any less", said Lynn.

"On the contrary, I'm working more, but just not getting paid as much for each procedure. It's gotten terrible over the past two or three years. Managed care continues to take over more companies. Business looks upon it as a way to reduce their overall expenditures for healthcare; patients look upon it as a way to save on premiums they have to pay. But in the medical profession, we just see it as a way for the insurance companies and our patients to get away with paying us less for the same procedures that we have been doing for years.

It's also taking away people's right to choose their personal physician as they had always done in the past. People used to pick doctors by reputation ... on referral from friends and family. Now to get to a specialist, you can only be referred by your *primary care physician*, and only to a specialist that participates in the plan if you choose an HMO.

It's nothing short of *blackmail:* you either belong to the plan, or you get no business. And when you join the plan, you are agreeing to take less for everything you do.

I tell you, Honey, they are judge and jury and appeals court all rolled up into one: they set the fees, adjudicate the fees and tell you 'no' almost 100% of the time when you appeal their low payments."

"You've been telling me about this for some time, but I didn't think it was this bad. I can certainly see why you seem to be more irritable these days when you come home from the office."

"Almost daily we're being solicited by new plans moving into the area. It's become like *alphabet soup* trying to keep up with their names and the tenets of each plan. We're literally forced to sign up with almost any plan that comes along promising to be a 'player' in the local market. If they do get a major contract with some local industry, and we don't belong ... well, we're dead in the water.

And in addition to reducing fees, they are impossible to communicate with. And they delay payment under the guise of the claim being *in review*. The big organizations in medicine are relatively powerless against them.

Honey, I tell you, as long as there is one doctor willing to sign these contracts, we'll never win the battle. One of these days, it'll be all-out war between them and us. Some days I'd just like to quit and do something else!"

Jack threw himself into his chair in obvious frustration.

"Jack, I know this is all very disconcerting. But tell me, why is Dave Fortner doing so well? Everyone says he's making a fortune with these new laparoscopic procedures. What's his secret?"

He confided the content of the meeting held earlier in the day concerning Dave Fortner.

"I've got to get working on that as soon as I can. It needs to be put to rest ... one way or the other."

CHAPTER 4

Midsouth—August 2005

The box of premium cigars was on Bill's desk when he returned. On the box was a card that read: "With continuing appreciation for your help with the *project*."

It was signed: ***From S & D***, initials that he recognized all too well.

"I wonder when and how this will all end?"

He reached into his desk drawer for his Tums.

Chapter 5

▼

Midsouth—October 24, 2005

The "Code Blue" team consisted of a designated physician on duty from the Emergency Department, his head nurse, personnel from the I.C.U., and respiratory therapy. The I.C.U. team brought the "crash cart" containing all the drugs and apparatus necessary to save a life in distress.

"Epi given" shouted the nurse to Dr. Walters, the emergency room physician now in charge of running the "code".

"She's bradying down again", he replied as he watched her pulse rate drop down again into the thirties, a critically slow rate that can be deadly when paired with a dropping blood pressure.

"One mg. of atropine", he ordered. The rate slowly began to increase ... temporarily, but then quickly fell back to its original level.

"Let's go ahead and intubate" he instructed the nurse anesthetist who had been in charge of administering sedation during the ERCP procedure. This meant placing a breathing tube into the patient's windpipe in order to insure adequate oxygenation.

"Dr. Walters!

Take a look at this right away" the anesthetist said, while pointing to the patient's mouth.

"Damn!

She must be having some type of allergic reaction. Her tongue and pharynx are all edematous."

"I can't get a tube in there ... it's impossible to see the vocal cords. You'd better call for an anesthesiologist and a surgeon stat."

"And get me a **Rapid-Trach** right away ... or we're going to lose her right now." **Rapid-Trach** is a device that allows placement of a small tube directly into the windpipe just below the ***Adam's apple*** using a needle-like instrument.

"Give her 50mg. of diphenhydramine stat, followed by one gram of Solu-Medrol.

And let's get a blood gas too", he yelled in the direction of the respiratory therapist.

The therapist immediately opened a blood oxygen sampling kit and felt for the patient's radial (wrist) pulse in an attempt to draw the arterial blood sample.

"Dr. Walters, I can't feel a pulse!"

The heart rate monitor that had been beeping in conjunction with the patient's pulse suddenly went silent ... verifying the therapist's statement.

There was no longer any pulse present.

"She's in asystole. Start CPR."

The nurses from I.C.U. standing at the periphery of the room quickly approached the patient and began chest compressions.

Precious time was ticking away. Seconds turned to minutes and still no surgeon appeared. The anesthesiologist was en route, but Dr. Walters would have to do something fast.

"Hand me the **Rapid-Trach** kit ... ***stat***."

He proceeded with its placement. It took more than three minutes to place and secure it; then several more minutes to make certain it was in good position. Finally, the pulse oximeter indicated that the patient was getting oxygen into the bloodstream, but not at normal levels.

The anesthesiologist arrived and assessed the situation.

"Good job with the trach", he said to Dr. Walters. He then inspected the patient's throat.

"I can see your problem. Any idea what the reaction was from?"

Dr. Walters and the nurse anesthetist recounted all the drugs that had been given, but the etiology remained obscure.

"And there has been no apparent response to the diphenhydramine or steroids," Dr Walters added.

The latest blood gas results returned and indicated that the patient's oxygen levels were low and acid products elevated, attesting to the gravity of the situation.

The CPR continued as additional drugs were given in an attempt to reverse the worsening situation.

The EKG improved slightly with the additional medications ... but again only temporarily. And the blood pressure was almost unobtainable. In essence, there was no effective cardiac output.

"She's in EMD. Let's start an Isuprel drip. And get an external pacemaker ready."

Electromechanical dissociation ... EMD ... is a condition where there is electrical heart activity apparent on the EKG, but no effective output by the heart. In essence, the patient is dead if the pressure cannot be rapidly restored.

Dr. Matheny, the anesthesiologist, watched as the Isuprel was given. There was no response. The pacemaker was applied and still no blood pressure could be obtained.

"Her pupils are beginning to dilate."

"Repeat the Epi and Atropine ... and give an amp of calcium gluconate", shouted Dr. Walters.

"Hurry, we're losing her."

There was anguish in his tone, reflecting his ... and everyone's ... inability to help the patient in this obscure situation ... a situation made only worse by the fact that she was young and had only come in for a diagnostic test.

Another ten minutes quickly passed as the CPR continued, and multiple drugs were administered and re-administered several times.

Meanwhile, Russ and Kevin stood helpless on the sidelines as the scenario played itself out. They were unable to intercede or affect the outcome in any way.

Finally, at 2:14 P.M., Dr. Walters looked at the others.

"I'm afraid she's gone. Mark this as the official time of death." The others tacitly concurred.

Turning to Kevin, he said: "I'm sorry. We did everything we could. What do you think went wrong?"

Kevin was stupefied.

"I don't know. We've done dozens ... perhaps a hundred of these procedures without any significant problems. From what you've told us, it sounds like some type of allergic reaction. But I haven't a clue what she would be allergic to. She didn't list any allergies to medications, and the ones we used are all routine to this procedure."

Of course, he didn't mention the special vial ... but then it too had been used many times before without incident.

Kevin knew there would have to be an investigation. This would be a medical examiner's case with an obligatory autopsy, since the death had occurred in the hospital while the patient was undergoing a procedure, and the cause of death not readily apparent.

And she was only forty-three years old!

Kevin eyed Russ standing at the periphery of the room. They both knew that this could spell big trouble for the *project* ... if not its end, unless they handled it properly. Unless they got the right medical examiner ... a member of their own team to perform the post-mortem exam ... all their efforts could be jeopardized.

They had known all along that this day could come ... perhaps even would come ... and they had prepared a contingency plan ... one that they hoped never to have to use.

Russ slipped out of the room and quickly put in a call to the in-house *project* leader. Someone needed to activate damage control immediately.

CHAPTER 6

▼

Midsouth—October 25, 2005

Mike detested special requests, especially when it involved performing autopsies ... and particularly under such stressful circumstances. He hadn't been fond of performing the procedure even as a resident; the special area that he was going into ... hematologic pathology ... rarely required autopsy specimens. But performing autopsies had been a requisite of the training program, and it was a requisite of being a part of his department, where work had to be shared.

And of course, it was a ***special request.***

When he heard the circumstances of the death, and that Kevin Bledsoe and Russ Callahan were involved, he knew he would have to assemble his "team". The responsibility for salvaging the situation on behalf of the ***project*** members would rest entirely on his shoulders.

He entered the autopsy suite and found the deceased lying on the prosector's table. His assistants had already performed all the preliminary preparations, and assembled the paperwork for him to review and complete.

Mike knew he would need to be extremely diligent in following all the prescribed steps for a procedure being done under such circumstances. There could be no short cuts. Everyone would be watching and waiting for his results ... his final opinion. And there would be reviews of his findings if there were any disputes from any side.

Legal ramifications were a high probability in such a case. Malpractice carriers for the physicians involved and the medical center had already requested records of the proceedings and would anticipate a copy of Mike's final report. The hospital risk management team had assigned the case a high priority.

He reviewed the patient's history, and then launched into the task at hand. He had a triple goal to accomplish: 1) determine the cause of death and present his findings to the coroner's office 2) protect the ***project*** without jeopardizing his own situation or presenting any "red flags" to the reviewing authorities should that eventuate 3) be able to assure the Code Blue team that they had done everything possible to save the patient's life.

The diener assisting him was part of his "team" and understood the implications of this being a ***project*** patient. He knew that his special help ... no matter what that required him to do ... would mean an extra deposit in his private bank account at the end of the month.

Mike began with a description of the body, as it lay naked on the dissecting table. He spoke into a voice-activated microphone that hung suspended over the table.

"The body is that of a Caucasian female consistent with the given age of forty-three years. The length is sixty-five inches and the weight one hundred and forty pounds. Hair color: blond. Eyes: brown. Livor mortis is present. There is no evidence of external torso trauma. A tracheotomy tube is in place."

Prior to beginning the dissection of the internal organs, his assistant took samples of body fluids, including blood and urine. He would handle them just as Mike had requested, making appropriate adjustments as necessary.

The standard Y-incision followed, exposing the chest and abdominal cavities and the organs contained within. They were systematically removed, weighed, and sampled.

The scalp was then incised and peeled forward to expose the cranium. The diener used a special saw to cut the bony cranium, exposing the vault containing the brain. It was removed, weighed, and sampled like the other organs.

That was the part that Mike had always hated the most ... and he was glad when it was finished. He detested the dehumanization of the person being examined when the facial tissue was literally inverted on itself as the scalp was peeled forward. He was always relieved when it had been restored to its natural state.

The final maneuver, necessitated by the history in this particular case, was examination of the mouth, tongue and neck. He would examine the tracheostomy site carefully to assure that there had been no error in its performance.

There was severe edema of the tongue and vocal cords as had been noted by the resuscitation team. The tracheostomy tube, which had been left undisturbed, was in good position in the trachea. The trachea below the tube appeared normal. Samples were taken from the areas of edema for analysis.

With that done, Mike's assistant restored the body to the pre-dissection state, and readied it for transport to the funeral home for burial preparation.

His initial job was done.

The more tedious and time-consuming part of the examination would be the preparation and evaluation of the collected materials, including making and interpreting microscopic slides, analyzing tissue and fluid samples, including utilizing electron microscopy and DNA sampling.

That data then had to be collated and interpreted and a final conclusion reached as to the cause of death. Those results then had to be promulgated to all necessary and interested parties.

And for Mike, there was the devilish task of making sure that everything remained consistent with maintaining the viability of the *project*, all the while not attracting the attention of outsiders who would undoubtedly review his work.

* * * *

"Everything here is under control", Mike reported to the damage control coordinator.

"Good. We're counting on you to bring us through this little setback. I'll notify the others."

* * * *

Evansville, N.C.—August 2000

Life in Evansville had been good to Mike Herman. Though born in Athens, Greece, his family had emigrated to the United States when he was only three years old. So the U.S. was essentially the only home that he had ever known.

He remembered nothing about Athens or his scant years there; the family had never returned after their arrival in the U.S. He only knew that the family name had been shortened from Hermanopoulos to Herman ... and his given name Americanized from Miklos to Michael.

Mike, as he was usually called ... even though he personally preferred Michael ... had grown up in Philadelphia, where his parents owned and operated the *Athena* restaurant. Though the menu included many Greek items, they advertised themselves as "a Mediterranean dining experience."

The business had been eminently successful for the Herman family. Mike's father, Dimitri, hoped that Mike ... the only son ... would one day join him in the business and ultimately take over the operation.

But Mike had chosen the medical profession.

His Uncle John (Ianni) was a family practitioner in Philadelphia whom Mike had always admired. From an early age, Mike aspired to attend Jefferson Medical School in Philadelphia, his uncle's *alma mater*.

If accepted, he decided that he would live at home and help out with the business, when possible, until he finished training. He owed his family that much at least, for providing him the opportunity to complete his education.

Mike earned a B.S. in Biology at the University of Pennsylvania, *cum laude*. Accepted at all three of the medical schools to which he applied, including Jefferson, he of course selected the latter. Initially, he had planned to become a family practitioner ... and perhaps even join his uncle in practice.

But during his second year of school, his career path took a sudden and unexpected turn during his Pathology rotation. He became interested in the subject of hematology and blood banking. With the enthusiastic endorsement of the department chairman, a summer rotation was arranged ... and his career choice was sealed.

Following graduation from medical school, he accepted a six-year residency program at Jefferson that would ultimately lead to his being a specialist in Pathology *and* Hematology and Blood Banking. The sixth and final year would be devoted entirely to the latter sub-specialty, making him one of few pathologists in the country with such credentials.

As his tenth year at Jefferson was finally drawing to a close, he decided that he had had enough of long northern winters. While searching for potential practice sites, he found an ad placed by Midsouth Regional Medical Center in a specialty newsletter, seeking someone with his credentials. The search firm put him in touch with Midsouth and a visit to Evansville, North Carolina was quickly arranged.

Ralph Gordon greeted Mike at the airport and escorted him to a social hour where he was introduced to the other members of the Pathology Department. The following morning, he was given a tour of the medical center, followed by a luncheon in his honor, attended by several department chairmen and by Bill Smithson.

Bill outlined the center's plans for future expansion that included a new outpatient blood banking facility and a special hematology lab. He sought Mike's input on several aspects of the plan in an effort to test his depth of knowledge on the subject.

Both sides were duly impressed. Mike later met with Bill and the Pathology Department chairman to discuss their financial package and proposed timetable for starting. It appeared to be a good fit for both parties.

By the time his plane touched down in Philadelphia later that afternoon, Mike was sold on Midsouth and decided he would take the position if offered. Bill Smithson, realizing a golden opportunity in Mike Herman's almost immediate availability, and superb credentials, called the following morning and extended him the offer.

Mike quickly accepted.

Following completion of his training program on June 30, he would be off to Evansville and bid farewell to the cold Pennsylvania climate forever.

*   *   *   *

Evansville, N.C.—August 2004

Now four years after his arrival in Evansville, Mike was firmly established in the Midsouth pathology department. His extensive investment of time and energy in establishing a new hematology lab for the hospital, and an outpatient reference hematology/blood bank facility, had resulted in their becoming model programs for the state and the southeast region.

While Mike's main responsibilities and interests were directed toward hematologic problems, he was still required to perform other duties of that department such as autopsies and surgical cuttings, both particularly loathsome tasks.

He preferred doing what he knew best … what he was more comfortable with … what he could claim expertise in … where he was in total control. He knew how to run a business as he had been taught well by his parents.

In spite of a rather intense work schedule, Mike had made time for occasional social activities. He preferred not to be labeled anti-social and he hated the word "nerd" … a term that had more than once been used to describe him during his college and medical training days.

His family maintained a home near the Delaware River in Buck's County, Pennsylvania, but had never owned a boat, or a cottage along the river itself. His only recollection of a water activity while growing up was the summer that his parents rented a cottage at Cape May, New Jersey.

Mike quickly became a water enthusiast after moving to Evansville, having been invited to try water skiing by one of the other doctors in his department. He found it a great way to enjoy the sunny south.

He particularly enjoyed looking back at the harsh Pennsylvania winters, laughing and thumbing his nose at Punxatawney Phil every Groundhog Day when the furry creature invariably proclaimed six more weeks of winter!

After his first year there, he had purchased a twenty-two foot fiberglass runabout and secured a berth at the marina on Lake Sydney, York County's premier water playground that had come into being about forty years earlier with the damming of the Pokwatonk River.

* * * *

She had been alone at the marina that day, sitting on the terrace enjoying the afternoon sun. Her ample silhouette projected across the deck towards where Mike sat.

He didn't recognize her at first. But something about her prompted him to strike up a conversation … a break from his usual bashful habit.

"We've met before, but I'm embarrassed to say that I don't remember where. And please … that's not just a come-on line."

She took his hand in hers, smiled demurely, and said in her finest southern drawl:

"Why Dr. Herman, I'm surprised that you remember me at all, since pathologists rarely visit the radiology department."

"Please, it's Mike", he retorted.

"Now I remember! I had a meeting with Dr. Callahan several weeks ago about some clinical correlation matters, and you were there. That is where we met, isn't it?"

"Why yes. I'm so pleased that you remembered."

"What do you do in the department?"

"Actually, I started out as an x-ray tech a number of years ago, but now I'm a department supervisor, so I do mostly administrative work. Some days I'm not sure if that's good or bad. I used to work a straight eight-hour day and was then free to go home. The bad feature was that I had to change shifts frequently.

Now I don't change shifts, but my hours are much more irregular and unpredictable. I do a lot of preparatory work for Dr. Callahan's meetings, like the one you attended when we met."

"Well, enough about your hospital duties. Tell me, what is a pretty girl like you doing at the lake alone? That is ... if you don't mind my getting personal?

Uh, that is ... assuming that you are alone?

Oh! That's a terrible assumption on my part!"

The words were barely across his lips when he thought to himself what an incredibly stupid thing it had been to say.

She saved him the embarrassment of an apology with a quick response.

"As a matter of fact, I am. I frequently come here for lunch when I'm not working. The view of the lake from here is so beautiful. And I just live a few miles away."

"It is pretty, isn't it?

And if you don't mind my saying so, it's even lovelier with you gracing the deck."

Mike suddenly didn't know what powerful force had inspired his thoughts. It wasn't like him to say such things, and never to a stranger.

"Listen", he added.

"I've got a boat ... why don't we make an afternoon of it on the lake?

Do you ski?"

She launched into her past history of repeated attempts and failures at skiing, but finally added:

"I'd love to give it another try if you're willing to put up with me. I know how to drive a boat, so I think it'll be safe for you to ski at least."

"Great", said Mike.

"And I don't want to get too personal, but ... are you married, or do you have a steady boyfriend?"

"I was married ... but I've been divorced for quite a while now. And I don't see anyone regularly."

"I'm going to embarrass myself hopefully one last time.

I still don't know your name."

"It's Danielle ... Danielle Morgan."

"What a lovely name", he thought to himself.

Danielle Morgan. He repeated it over and over in his head. It had a musical quality like a refrain in a song you can't forget.

Danielle Morgan.

Danielle Morgan!

"Well, Danielle, let's not waste any more of this gorgeous day just standing here and talking. I'm going to make a skier out of you this afternoon."

He offered her his hand and led the way down the steps to his boat slip. Each silently thought that they had to get to know more about the other ... and this promised to be a great start. Today, they would enjoy the sunshine and water ... and see where fate led them from there.

* * * *

The afternoon vanished in an instant. Mike and Danielle spent the day like two old friends, although he *knew* as he watched her trying to ski that he wanted her to be more than just a friend.

Dusk beckoned, forcing them to yield to the coming darkness.

"How about dinner ... that is, if you don't have other plans?" he suddenly blurted out.

"Mike, I'd love to ... it's been such a wonderful day ... but, can I take a rain check? I have some things that I have to do tonight. But I want you to promise that you'll call me soon."

She didn't mention another engagement, but he inferred that she probably had a date that evening. He was hurt ... but then, why wouldn't a beautiful woman like this have a suitor at her door every night?

He didn't want to pry any further, but he was sure that he had to see her again ... and soon. Something had stirred in his most personal male parts ... something that he had not felt before.

And he liked the feeling. This was a person ... a body ... that he surely must come to know better.

"Good night, Danielle. I promise that I'll call you very soon. It was a lovely day."

She kissed him lightly on the cheek and then quickly disappeared into the gathering darkness.

* * * *

Danielle departed for home, leaving Mike wondering about her plans for the evening. She had been purposefully vague ... it's best to leave men guessing ... that's what *sister* had always taught her.

She arrived home and quickly set about her usual evening routine: a cup of freshly brewed coffee, reading the mail and the afternoon paper, and watching TV.

Her marriage to Bruce Morgan had survived for four years; she had now spent two years alone. He was a stockbroker in one of Evansville's largest investment firms. But career plans had gotten in both of their ways, and divorce had become the only logical solution for a relationship whose only common denominator for their final year together had been their street address.

Now she relied on *sister's* choice of men for her dates.

"*Gizmo*", she said to her attentive feline companion, "I hope that *sister* will like him. I need to call and let her know about my day."

Gizmo, a seal point Balinese, brushed her tail against Danielle's leg, looked at her with her almond shaped blue eyes, and purred as if to indicate that she understood and agreed with her assessment of the situation.

CHAPTER 7

▼

Evansville, N.C.—August 2004

When the phone rang, she was just getting out of the shower, and had to run half-naked into the bedroom to answer it.

"Hi, Sis", said the voice on the other end.

It was Danielle.

"I've made contact with him just like you asked me to do. He's kind of cute and I think he likes me. I could fall for him if you'd let me."

"That may come later. Just stick to the plan for right now until he's securely ours. When are you going to see him again?"

"He's supposed to call me soon. He even asked me to dinner after we went skiing at Lake Sydney this afternoon."

"Well, what happened at dinner?"

"I didn't go. I thought you'd prefer that I didn't act too interested right away."

"Are you crazy? You could be accomplishing a lot more if you were with him right now. You could be finding out some of those things we talked about.

Don't leave so many things to chance in the future, Danielle.

Do you understand me?" she added in a hostile tone.

"Of course I do" she replied.

"You're my older sister and you always know the best way to handle things and people ... especially men. I always try to do what you say."

"Then follow my plan. You'll have plenty of time to use him as you see fit if you just do what I tell you.

I just need to ensure that he'll be there when I need him. Now get to work."

Sister slammed the phone down and returned to the bathroom.

"Damn younger generation. It's so hard to get them to use a little common sense when necessary."

Chapter 8

▼

Evansville, N.C.—July 2005

"I hear from my sources that I was the main topic of discussion that several of our surgeons had with Jack Davidson after the surgical review committee today. They may be on to something."

"You just leave everything to me. I have my ways of taking care of things."

"That's what I'm afraid of."

Dave quickly hung up the phone.

* * * *

Dave Fortner had been associated with Midsouth for over twenty years. Following graduation from a small upstate New York college, he had completed medical school and surgical residency training in Boston. And after nine years in Massachusetts, and a lifetime in the Northern U.S.… he had had enough of the frigid winters and generally intemperate climate.

Midsouth had been waging a fairly intense recruitment campaign for physicians in a variety of specialties, including general surgery. Evansville's growth rate was predicted to continue at or above the national average for the foreseeable future. Dave was offered a guaranteed a salary for the first year, along with an office and secretarial help for the first six months free of charge.

The temperate weather and preponderance of sunny days in Evansville had afforded him the opportunity to accomplish what he could not do while a resident: get his unrestricted pilot's license, and purchase his first plane … a used Cessna 172 … thanks to a brisk first year in business.

Dave met Sarah Coleman when she came to work as a registered nurse in the Surgical Intensive Care Unit at Midsouth. She initially had a "significant other", but following their breakup, things began to change.

With her promotion to head nurse, she began accompanying him on rounds … and at the end of those rounds inviting him to join her for coffee in the nurse's lounge. His inherent shyness gradually gave way to her charm.

Following a series of lackluster dates, Sarah boldly suggested to Dave that she would love for him to take her flying … that she had always wanted to see the Evansville/York County area from the air, and that she would especially enjoy the experience in his company.

Short excursions gave way to daylong trips, followed by overnight stays at a secluded spot near the coast that Dave had discovered years earlier.

It was there that they shared their first intimate encounter. It had seemed to him a natural progression of their relationship.

Sarah Coleman, thirty-five and blond, with a size eight figure, was a catch for any man … and especially for the shy, reserved Dave Fortner.

But true colors are often revealed only after the prey is caught in a web; only when extrication is virtually impossible without the payment of a dear price … often one's life or livelihood.

* * * *

Midsouth—March 2004

Their romantic encounters had remained brief, although intense at times, until finally Dave asked Sarah to accompany him to a meeting in Honolulu. She was thrilled with the idea immediately, never having been to Hawaii. And she knew that it would fit into her plans perfectly.

She was now Vice President of Patient Affairs at Midsouth, so arranging an extended absence on short notice was easily accomplished.

"Let's be sure and leave hospital business in Evansville", he admonished her.

"I want you to enjoy Hawaii … and me."

She had just enough time to make *other* necessary arrangements.

* * * *

San Francisco, California—April 2004

Rather than take an arduous non-stop flight to Honolulu, Dave suggested they leave two days early and stopover in San Francisco, a place neither had previously visited. Approaching their hotel near Fisherman's Wharf, they could see wisps of fog beginning to steal into the bay, shrouding the Golden Gate Bridge.

"What a lovely view" Sarah remarked to him.

In their room, Sarah disappeared momentarily into the bathroom, and reappeared wearing only a transparent peignoir.

"Talk about a lovely view.

San Francisco has nothing on you!"

"I've waited impatiently all day to do this", she said as she put her arms around him and gave him a lingering kiss.

Now they could both feel his manhood coming alive. He was unable to control his erection any longer. They disrobed each other quickly, fully … the game playing was at an end.

Now this man who had found little time for women in his younger days was unbridled. Passion seethed from his entire being, matching hers stroke for stroke. He touched her in ways that even she had not felt before; together they explored sexual positions that they had only read about in books.

And while they explored every inch of each other's bodies, he repeatedly told her how much he had always wanted her.

"Is he trying to tell me he loves me?

God, he's so marvelous in bed." She briefly considered abandoning her plans.

But old memories demand revenge. Plans made must be accomplished … in spite of momentary distracting pleasures. For now she would just lie in his arms and savor the moment. The outside world and its problems would have to wait.

The following morning found the couple languishing in bed like honeymooners after their wedding. After another intense lovemaking session, they set out to enjoy their day in the bay area.

As they crossed the Golden Gate Bridge en route to Marin County, Dave took furtive glances at the lovely woman riding next to him and tried to imagine how life would be with her by his side. He smiled as he imagined the things that they might do together as a family … and at the things that he longed to do to her again and again. Lingering thoughts of last night and this morning's love making sessions were etched into his brain like a lurid tattoo.

And the satisfied look on her face convinced him that she felt the same way too. He couldn't remember a time that he had seen her so content, so apparently engrossed only in the present.

"Sarah, I'm really glad that you agreed to come with me on this trip. I don't think I've ever enjoyed myself, or anyone else more."

She tried to put from her mind the real motive for accompanying him, and for once she succeeded. At the hotel that night they repeated their intimacy lessons, both beginning to wonder who was the teacher and who was the student, but each embracing the homework without complaint.

Morning would come early, and their plane awaited them just after nine a.m.

* * * *

Honolulu, Hawaii—April 2004

United 73 departed San Francisco on schedule. With the time gain between California and the fiftieth state, it wasn't even noon when the jumbo jet touched down at Honolulu International Airport.

It was a bright sunny afternoon on Oahu, so Dave suggested they take a drive to the north shore before settling into their hotel for the night. He negotiated the rented convertible out of the airport parking area onto the Kamehameha ... "Kam" Highway ... and turned toward Pearl City.

"I want to show you some of my favorite places, and stop and let you sample some fresh pineapple ... if you've never had it fresh from the field, you don't know just how good pineapple can taste."

He reached over and gave her a light kiss on the cheek, then accelerated away from the stoplight.

"This is going to be so much fun having you along."

She snuggled up next to him and placed her head on his shoulder.

"I'm really having a good time, too. I've never taken a vacation like this before. I plan to enjoy every minute of it with you."

There was no hint in the inflection of her voice that she meant anything but what she said.

The temperature hovered in the mid-eighties; a light trade wind blew, and scattered clouds lightly draped the Koolau's in the distance as they made their way toward Pearl City en route to Wahiawa and the North Shore. Though it had been several years since his last visit to the islands, he drove with a strange familiarity.

There had been an improvement in some of the roads, several high rise buildings now loomed along the skyline, and the impressive Aloha Bowl sat incongruously adjacent to Pearl Harbor. Otherwise, it remained as familiar as Hospital Drive in Evansville.

"It's hard to imagine how this must have looked on the morning of December 7, 1941."

In the distance they could see Ford Island, the small island in the center of the harbor, around which were moored most of the ships sunk on the morning of the Japanese attack.

The *Arizona Memorial* lay adjacent to Ford Island. Military and commercial watercraft shuttled about the harbor as if unaware of their historic surroundings.

"We'll come back to the memorial another day", he said. Sarah had indicated she would like to visit it sometime during their stay.

Dave avoided the new "interstate" highways that had been constructed since his last visit. A misnomer, they obviously didn't lead to any other state, but utilized government funds so designated. They would take the H-1 back to town since it would be faster, as they were sure to be tired.

At Wheeler Air Force Base, Dave veered off to pass by the entrance to Schofield Barracks, the Army base strafed by Japanese planes as they exited Kolekole Pass at the rear of the base property. The pass is the V-shaped formation in the Waianae Mountain range; through it the Japanese were able to make a low-level surprise approach to the islands.

"It's mind-boggling to think that so many planes could fly across the island without detection.

Today, they would be seen approaching from hundreds of miles away. And a single modern jet could probably have taken out the entire Japanese fleet, considering how primitive their weapons were. Their planes would never even have left the decks of their carriers.

The Army actually had a radar installation on the northwest corner of the island. But the concept of radar was new and not well understood by the soldiers in charge of the facility that morning. They actually saw the planes coming and relayed the information to the Watch Officer. But, he decided it must be a squadron of B-17's that was expected in from the mainland that morning.

Big mistake!"

Sarah interrupted him. She found him to be a kid when it came to the history of Hawaii, WWII and of airplanes.

"How do you know so much about all of this?"

She feigned interest in his continuing the story although she longed to see the inside of their hotel room ... and to feel the gentle caress of this exciting man she had found.

"My first visit here taught me about the history of the islands and the people, and it made me acutely aware of the place of aviation in war, especially World War II. With my interest in flying, and in Hawaii, I was naturally compelled to continue to study the two."

He turned north and rejoined the Kam highway, approached the Dole pineapple pavilion and turned in.

"But enough about all that for now. How about sharing some fresh pineapple? Then we'll head back to town and the hotel."

The native fruit fresh from the fields was unlike anything that came from a can ... Dole labeled or not.

"Put just a little salt on it. It makes it taste even sweeter."

"This is a little bit of heaven. I've never had any fresh fruit that tasted better", Sarah concluded.

Dave sensed that she was tired, and had heard enough about Hawaiian history and airplanes and pineapple for one day. So he pointed the car towards the H-1 and made the trip back to Waikiki in half the time it had taken them to Wahiawa from the airport.

"Well, here's our home for the next week" he said as they approached the **Royal Hawaiian** hotel.

"Around here she's called the 'pink palace'" ... a reference to the exterior color of the building. The hotel was one of the original three major hotels at Waikiki Beach, dating from the war years.

"If it's o.k. with you, can we just get some dinner downstairs. I'm too tired to go out tonight", she whispered to Dave as they settled their things in the room.

They had a quick, albeit excellent dinner at the in-house Italian *ristorante*. But the day had been long and each longed for the privacy of their bedroom.

Sarah reappeared from the bathroom wearing only a towel. She went straight to Dave, kissed him fully on the lips as her hand slid to his crotch. She immediately discarded the towel and lay naked on the bed for him.

Tonight there was no warming up. Their rehearsal at the wharf hotel was the only prelude to the pleasures that the night would bring. As flesh quickly melded into one, their arms and legs intertwined.

She gasped, unable to fully get a breath of air ... and enough of him. They clung to each other as though afraid that someone was waiting to separate them.

Dave smiled to himself. Thoughts that he was falling in love filled his head as he slowly surrendered to the fatigue that now consumed his body. And Sarah watched him sleep ... and considered her next move.

Pleasure ... yes. Love ... perhaps.

But promises must be fulfilled!

This was going better than she had planned.

*   *   *   *

He arose early the following morning and quickly dressed for his meeting being held in the hotel's main ballroom downstairs. He approached the bed and gave her a kiss.

"Shhh! Don't get up. I'm going to my meeting. You get some rest and I'll see you about noon. Be thinking about what you'd like to do this afternoon ... the day is all yours. I'll order you up some breakfast for nine a.m."

She smiled as he disappeared through the door.

She reached for the phone. She already had preliminary plans for more important matters that needed her full and undivided attention, and she needed to make some quick calls. The afternoon, she knew, would take care of itself.

CHAPTER 9

▼

Midsouth—July 2005

"And finally, I hope that each and every one of you will give serious consideration to the nursing positions that are available here at Midsouth Regional Medical Center.

It has been my privilege to be here with you today. If you have any further questions, Ms. Coleman and I will be available to answer them at the conclusion of the program."

With these remarks, Bill rested while the program concluded, glad to have fulfilled his latest … and hopefully last … obligation to Sarah.

She approached him afterward.

"Thanks again for your help, Bill."

She leaned over and continued talking in a whisper.

"Is everything going o.k. with the *project* as far as you are concerned?"

He nodded affirmatively, the while looking around the room at the applicants and smiling.

"Do you really plan to continue with this?

Haven't you asked enough of me already?"

She smiled at the others in the room as she firmly whispered back for his ears only.

"I'll say when enough is *enough*. Until then, just keep doing what I ask … that is, unless you'd like to consider the possible alternatives."

Bill clearly understood the veiled threat just uttered and said no more.

*   *   *   *

July 27, 2005
Midsouth

The surgery department met monthly on the fourth Wednesday at noon. Since it was a luncheon meeting, attendance was generally good. Jack chaired the meeting.

He had initially considered bringing up the Fortner matter to the body considering the infrequency of their meetings, but had decided against it. If his impression was correct ... that jealousy on the part of a few members of the department was the main reason behind the allegation ... then the fewer people involved the better.

Not that he and Dave Fortner were the best of friends ... they occasionally worked together on big cases requiring the assistance of a colleague. But Dave had always been willing to help. Jack considered him competent and technically adept, and above all ... trustworthy. He just couldn't imagine him doing something patently illegal.

Jack wanted *not* to find anything amiss ... to have no reason to pursue the allegation. He decided that he would undertake a private investigation of the matter, and only involve the committee as a whole if he found something to substantiate the allegations. He wanted to avoid it looking like a jealousy contest among surgery department members.

He would need help from Pathology and Radiology. He knew that Mike Herman would be out of town for a few days, so he decided that radiology would be the best place to start the investigation. Since everyone having gallbladder surgery would have had one or more radiologic studies before any operation, he would collect data from there and later match it up with reports from surgical pathology.

If he found nothing incriminating at that point, it would not be worthy of reporting to the surgery department or the surgical review committee. Instead, he would compile a report for the Executive Committee alone. He wouldn't want it to appear as though he had swept the whole affair under the rug. At the same time, he didn't want the whole world to be privy to the accusations. Once made, they are hard ... if not impossible ... to retract.

* * * *

He began in Radiology with Russ Callahan. Jack explained the nature of the problem, and the need for utmost discretion. Russ had agreed to provide him the information that he needed.

Danielle Morgan had been asked to gather the data for him. They scheduled a meeting for the following morning.

*   *   *   *

"Dr. Davidson, it's so nice to see you again." She flashed a smile.

"I hope that you and your family are all well?"

She had known Jack from his frequent visits to the department to review x-ray studies, and had met Lynn and the children at a hospital sponsored staff picnic.

"Danielle, it's nice to see you again. The family is just fine. Thank you for asking.

May I assume that Dr. Callahan has briefed you on what I need?"

"He indicated something about gallbladder studies, but beyond that he didn't go into any detail.

He just asked that I help you with whatever you need."

"As Chief of Surgery, I've been asked to prepare a report for the American College of Surgeons on the current use of a variety of diagnostic tests for gallbladder disease, and how they correlate with the new surgical procedures we are performing. They're trying to determine if we can judge ahead of time which procedure is indicated."

He hated telling **white lies** but knew that they were occasionally necessary to preserve confidentiality.

"So I will need copies of all gallbladder ultrasound tests, CT scans involving the hepatobiliary tree, HIDA scans, MRCP's and any ERCP studies done in the department over the past year.

That should include tests done for the Emergency Department and any private physicians' offices as well. And if you've already gotten pathology correlation, it would save me time not having to get it directly from them."

Jack knew that radiology routinely did these correlation studies, since it was an integral part of their ongoing accreditation requirements.

"Well, that's not asking for too much, now is it?" He smiled as he uttered the words, knowing that he was placing a major imposition on the radiology department, and Danielle in particular. Even with the aid of a computer, it could take quite a while to gather the information.

"Oh, and one final thing: I'd like to know if any of the reports were sent to physicians other than the one who ordered the test."

He could see by the look on her face that Danielle already felt overwhelmed.

"I'll do the best I can, but you know there could be an awful lot of tests results in one year. We're in the process of changing over part of our computer system, so it may take a week or two just to get enough results to get you started."

He hated waiting, but he understood. Computer updating was a fact of modern medicine.

"Thanks, Danielle. I know you'll do your best. Let me know when you have something."

* * * *

Russ Callahan had been Chairman of the Radiology Department at Midsouth for the preceding three years. A native of Montana, he had been recruited to Evansville during its high growth phase. Along with three other radiologists, they had founded the department that now had grown to fourteen members.

Now a senior member of the group, he had championed much of the department's early development and brought it to the high level of excellence it now enjoyed. His radiologic colleagues had rewarded him by electing him chairman of their department.

Russ was also the current Vice Chief of the Medical Staff, a position that would automatically promote him to Chief of Staff at the beginning of the following year. The two-year tenure job would place him at the head of the four hundred plus active and courtesy staff physicians that made up the medical workforce at Midsouth.

Russ had been married to Barbara for seventeen years. Bobbi, as she preferred to be called, was raised in Sparks, Nevada, a Reno suburb. She had gone to New Mexico after nurses training where she worked in the emergency department of the university hospital.

Russ was completing his radiology residency at the same institution; the two had been introduced by a mutual friend. They were married just prior to leaving Albuquerque for Evansville.

She had worked for a short time in the emergency department at Midsouth, but retired from nursing after becoming pregnant.

While she was proud of her husband's success and understood the sacrifices necessary on both of their parts that frequently accompany such achievement, she like most wives didn't like the fact that call nights now necessitated staying at the hospital as the volume of business grew and special procedures were added.

In addition, department meetings or Executive Committee meetings were almost weekly. And leadership retreats during the year required his being out of town for two or three days at a time.

What Russ had not planned on was **Linda** occupying a good deal of his time.

Linda Young had been an ultrasound tech in the radiology department for several years. Like most men, Russ couldn't help but notice her good looks and flirtatious manner. But he had managed to limit his association with her to harmless flirtation … until that one evening alone with her in the department led to hand holding and a shared kiss or two.

He knew it was wrong, but he also knew that it couldn't end there.

Russ arranged for Linda to attend an ultrasound update course at the American College of Radiology meeting that he would be attending in Dallas. The couple was able to secret themselves away for several nights, engaging in a torrid love affair. He surprised even himself by giving into such a sordid tryst. But then men are nothing more than little boys when it comes to being seduced by the opposite sex.

She was twenty-nine years of age, with raven black hair and blue eyes, with a figure that should well have graced the cover of the **Sports Illustrated Swimsuit Edition.**

Their rendezvous in Dallas was followed by intimate encounters in his call room at the hospital. Amazingly, their secret affair had managed to survive the scrutiny of the world and their co-workers for almost a year.

Such affairs, however, have a way of needing to progress … to mature … or to die.

She approached him slowly one evening while both were on duty alone.

"Russ, I need to talk to you privately whenever you have a few minutes."

He sensed the foreboding in her tone, and an unspoken urgency about her need to talk. As quickly as he concluded his dictation, he sought her out in the break room.

"Russ, we can't go on meeting like this. It's been almost a year and I can't bear the thought of having to go on being next to you and having to hide my feelings … not being able to touch you or be held by you when I want. We've never had more than a few hours together since our time in Dallas.

I love you, Russ. But I need you full time, not part time.

And I don't want to lose you."

He held his composure. Speechless, he stood and thought for a few moments. He knew this day would eventually come ... but like death, it is always too soon and generally unwelcome when it does arrive. They had discussed the possibility of his leaving Bobbi for her. But he wasn't prepared for such an upheaval at this moment. He was approaching the zenith of his career ... and such a move right now would generate much embarrassment and endless speculation ... things he would not welcome. And she would always be regarded as the "other woman" ... who had stolen him away from a lovely wife and two children. She would be forever branded a home wrecker.

He knew that the situation she now thrust upon him required tact and diplomacy from him ... here and now. He held her hand and spoke in a low gentle voice:

"Darling, you know how much I care for you and that I want to be with you always too. But let's get together this weekend at your place to discuss it when we both have the time. It's too important to talk about right here, right now.

I have an arteriogram to do in about ten minutes."

He gave her a soft kiss on the lips.

She knew that he was right and agreed to meet on Saturday. She returned his kiss.

"Get on back to work and I'll see you then", she said as she left the room.

Russ sighed a sigh of relief. He would have a few more days to formulate his next move.

Meanwhile, when Linda arrived home that evening, she decided to call her sister.

"I'll ask **sister** what she would do. She always knows how to handle things ... especially where men are concerned."

She lifted the phone from the cradle and placed the call.

Chapter 10

▼

Midsouth—August 2005

Jack Davidson thrived on the action areas of the hospital: the emergency department, the I.C.U., and especially the operating room ... his home in the hospital. These were the areas that got his adrenalin pumping; the areas that demanded excellence ... the areas where you had to be right the first time and every time ... if patients were to survive their illnesses.

He was good at what he did ... he knew it and accepted that others did as well ... and respected him for his abilities. He took time to listen to people's private problems and share personal stories. He was available to advise when asked, and listen when that was all that was required.

Jack loved walking into the I.C.U. each morning, especially when his favorite nurses were working ... *good* nurses who did their best in one of the tougher areas of the hospital in which to work.

"Good morning, Dr. Davidson. I'm still waiting for you to tell me you're ready to leave your wife and take *me* home."

It was Elaine's standard opening line. They would all share a laugh over a cup of coffee as she and the other nurses briefed him on his current I.C.U. patients.

Her comment went without a response. It was all part of the necessary diversions done to relieve the tension that was constantly building in this critical section of the hospital.

I.C.U. life is hard on nursing personnel. Days are generally filled with one life-threatening crisis after another, relieved only by the transfer of the patient to a regular nursing floor if improving ... or by death, a daily fact of life for I.C.U. nurses. Critically ill patients frequently die, no matter what the skill level of the physician in charge, or the dedication of the assigned nurse.

"Burnout" is a potentially serious affliction among the nurses assigned to the special care units. Transfer requests to other less stressful areas of the hospital ... or resignation ... had been a serious problem for the nursing administration at Midsouth as it had been in most similar size institutions. It had become a major cause of disruption of care, and major expense for the hospital due to having to retrain nurses to fill ever recurring vacancies.

As chairman of the I.C.U. committee, Jack had had the opportunity to work closely with the nursing staff on a number of critical issues, and specifically nursing burnout. Under his leadership, the I.C.U. committee had asked for and received permission from Midsouth administration to institute stress management classes for the I.C.U. nurses, and later for the emergency department nurses who suffered similarly.

The Psychology staff from Evansville State University, located on the northern border of town, conducted the classes. In its first year, the program increased retention of nursing personnel in the two areas by fifty per cent.

Jack was in total command in the operating room. He often thought back to his days as a surgical resident ... and later as a vascular surgical fellow ... to the many times when he had felt totally inadequate to handle particular situations. But several of his mentors perceived his latent abilities, and had succeeded in instilling in him the confidence that he now possessed.

Jack's former surgery department chairman, Mike DeLuca, had taken a special liking to him; they spent several months together when Jack rotated on his private service. Jack credited him with his transition to an extremely competent surgeon by the time he had completed the training program.

Gunther Harlowe, Jack's fellowship director, also took him under his direct tutelage during their year together and further enhanced his confidence. By the time Jack entered into practice, he was comfortable handling virtually any urgent problem as well as the routine.

"How great it would be to spend a few days working with them again", he thought. Jack and Lynn recently had had the opportunity to have lunch with Mike DeLuca and his wife while attending a meeting in St. Louis. They couldn't help but notice how age was overtaking him. And they were distressed at the recent announcement of his impending retirement.

"What a shame that future residents there won't have him for a teacher."

※ ※ ※ ※

"Dr. Davidson." The voice blared over the intercom into the O.R. dressing room.

"They're ready in room four", said the O.R. secretary.

Jack was instantly transported back to reality, and proceeded to the scrub sink to prepare for his next case.

Chapter 11

▼

Midsouth—July 2005

The pain had been subtle at first: just a nagging under her right rib cage that had persisted over several days and was especially annoying at night. She was bothered by the constant indigestion and belching that followed eating certain foods ... especially that Texas chili that her husband had made over the weekend. Over-the-counter medicines gave her only the briefest relief, if any.

Joyce Martin worked hard at the furniture plant. Her employer demanded faithful service from his employees and offered little latitude in granting time off for illness. So at the completion of her shift at seven p.m., she headed straight for the nearest emergency room ... at Midsouth.

"Hi Mrs. Martin, I'm Dr. Frank Li".

The emergency room physician sat and listened intently to her complaints, examined her abdomen, and then ordered a few tests. When they had been completed, he returned and sat down with her to discuss the results and propose treatment.

"It appears that you're having a gallbladder attack ... your ultrasound exam shows that you have gallstones.

I'm going to have the nurse give you some medication to control your pain, and several prescriptions that I want you to take.

But I also want you to follow up with our family practitioner on call ... Dr. Carl Hauser, since you don't already have a doctor here in town. He may want to do some additional tests or possibly even refer you to a gastroenterologist. Undoubtedly, he will send you to see a surgeon as well. You'll eventually have to get your gallbladder removed.

The nurse will return in a few minutes with the medications and prescriptions. She'll give you Dr. Hauser's office address and phone number. Call his office in the morning and tell the receptionist that I referred you for an urgent follow up appointment. If you should have any more problems before he can see you, we'll be happy to see you here again."

"What a great doctor", Joyce thought, as Frank Li exited her cubicle en route to his next patient.

* * * *

Frank Li was chairman of the Emergency Department at Midsouth. He had arrived in Evansville from California nine years earlier. Although born in Mainland China, his family had moved to the west coast when he was three. So despite his Oriental outward appearance, his speech and mannerisms were distinctly American.

Patients meeting him expected an authentic Oriental accent to accompany the Oriental name and almond eyes. They were pleased and surprised when he spoke with a slight Western drawl.

Frank had accepted the position of Chief of Emergency Services two years after his arrival at Midsouth when the former director, Dr. Mark Dowling, returned home to Michigan.

In addition to being on the committee that had helped recruit Frank Li, Jack had now worked with him on numerous E.R. cases, and the two had served together on the Executive Committee. They had become good friends almost instantly. Their wives, too, had become friends when they discovered they shared mutual interests in quilting and antique collecting.

The couples often spent weekends in town at each other's homes. The men respected each other's abilities and the couples cherished each other's friendship.

But sinister forces were at work to change all that in the near future.

Chapter 12

▼

Midsouth—September 7, 2005

Jack walked into the conference room where Danielle Morgan was awaiting his arrival.

"Good morning, Dr. Davidson. I've got some of the information you requested. But as I believe I mentioned to you about our computer system ... it's being upgraded and they don't have all the data reloaded yet.

I do have the gallbladder ultrasound reports for the first six months of the year. But the other reports ... the CT scans and HIDA scans ... that may take quite a while. And we only have a few MRCP's. The computer people promised us that it would only take two weeks for the switchover. But you know how that goes.

The new system will be completely digitized. The information you want will be simple to pull up on the new program since there'll be built-in software specifically for research and comparison data."

He could see the large stack of report copies that she had placed in a box for him. Surely that would be enough to keep him busy for quite a while.

"It looks like quite a lot already. Just let me know when you have more", he said, trying to remain polite.

He had hoped to collate all the data at one time, and then move on to pathology ... but he understood and thanked her for the reports.

"By the way, you did clear these with Dr. Callahan?" asked Jack before turning to leave, his arms filled with the paper laden box.

"I can assure you, he knows all about it."

Jack promised himself he would get to work analyzing the reports as soon as he could. In the meantime, he had a full day at the office.

CHAPTER 13

▼

Altamont, N.C.—1980

Childhood should be a time for fun, while parents hover close to offer comfort and protection and to teach and nurture.

But for the three young girls, the opposite had been true. The mere presence of their father instilled sheer terror in the trio of sisters ... a memory that carried across the years and continued to fill their days and nights with haunting thoughts and a burning desire for revenge ... against the father ... a physician and respected member of the community ... someone that the public would have thought incapable of perpetrating such abomination on anyone, especially his own progeny.

And there beside the father was a step-mother who failed to protect them from his wrath; a step-mother, educated, maternal, but an utter failure to the girls in the shadow of her spouse; a step-mother who enjoyed being a doctor's wife more than risking loss of social standing to protect her three helpless charges ... a decision that she would later regret following his death and their estrangement from her.

He had begun administering corporal punishment as soon as they were old enough to understand and learn. Activities planned by the father filled their days from morning to night; school, household chores, music lessons, and homework left virtually no room for play. And there was no satisfying his ever-increasing demands.

Whatever the activity, it could never be done to his satisfaction.

"You can always do better. Hard work builds character", he chanted in response to their every effort.

The lack of praise alone would have devastated most young children. But he would follow his sharp verbal assault with a whipping using his razor strap. And then the final insult: isolation in a dark closet, where no one was allowed to console the miscreant.

It continued relentlessly across the years, allowing the girls no apparent hope for escape. As a teenager, the eldest of the girls finally challenged her father ... even offering to accept punishment for her younger sisters, still too fragile to handle his berating.

He found her courage noble and occasionally accepted her offer ... but never lessened the punishment.

As they grew, the elder sister repeatedly reminded the younger two of her sacrifices on their behalf. And they pledged their loyalty should she need their help in the future.

It was a solemn pledge made in a time of desperation ... and one not to be forgotten or broken.

* * * *

And as the young girls had matured into womanhood, the thoughts and nightmares persisted. As the long nights of solitude eventually gave way to the dawn of a new day, so desperation was determined to find a solution ... a means to avenge their father's actions.

And *sister* would finally seek her siblings help to retaliate against the father for his cruel treatment during those harrowing years.

Chapter 14

▼

Midsouth—August 2005

Dave Fortner had been unquestionably the busiest surgeon at Midsouth for the past several years. His speed in the O.R. had not gone unnoticed by many of his colleagues. Some felt it unsafe, but there had been no reports of major complications. Faster surgery meant potentially lower infection rates ... and increased volume of cases meant increased revenue for the institution as well as Dave Fortner.

Dr. Fortner had developed a symbiotic relationship with Bill Smithson. Bill was only too happy to troubleshoot the occasional problem he encountered in the O.R. regarding equipment needs. He expedited new equipment requests for him in order to assure the steady cash flow that Dave so amply provided the institution.

Many staff members felt this represented unwarranted favoritism or pandering on the part of the administration, while others were more practical. Anyone generating the amount of revenue that Dave Fortner was currently feeding into the institution probably deserved special treatment.

Still others felt that there had to be more to the relationship ... implying something illegal.

If idle gossip is the elixir of life, then hospitals are intoxicated by it. The stories continued to circulate. Such stories usually play themselves out slowly and subtly ... but nevertheless disappear.

But this one wouldn't go away.

* * * *

Honolulu—April 2004

Life in Waikiki moves at a pace reminiscent of Manhattan's Broadway. This popular tourist site became famous following World War II. The tragedy that was **Pearl Harbor** catapulted the Hawaiian Islands into world prominence, with the unequaled beauty of its beaches, its sandy shores, and Diamond Head. The sedate Oahu of the 1940's had become the major tourist destination of the late twentieth century thanks to the advent of affordable jet travel.

The outer islands of Kauai and Maui continue to move more sedately, reminiscent of the days of the old kingdom ... before Hawaii had become an American protectorate, and eventually the fiftieth state.

Sarah remained secluded in their room, working on *her* plans while Dave attended his meeting. She occupied her time perusing sightseeing brochures she had acquired from the car rental agency and from the concierge desk in the hotel lobby.

One brochure featured Maui with a detailed article chronicling its main city, Lahaina, whaling capital of the Pacific in the 1800's, as well as stories and photographs of tropical golf courses such as Kapalua. Two pages were devoted to stories and pictures of Mt. Haleakala, the dormant volcano in the central part of the island, with its uncanny resemblance to lunar terrain.

But it was the feature article on **Hana**, a small village situated on the islands eastern end that captured her attention. By its very description, this town and its nearby remote beaches separated from the rest of the island by a two-hour drive over twisting roads was the very place that she had been seeking. This could be the site that would allow her to bring her plan together ... to see it set in motion.

It appeared perfect!

Sarah made several quick phone calls to the mainland. It was time to muster her forces.

* * * *

She was lounging on the *lanai,* addressing post cards when he returned.

"Isn't it fun to let people know what a great time you're having while they're back home working?"

He detected a slightly wicked tone in her voice and chose to ignore her remark.

Realizing it had fallen on deaf ears, she continued.

"Well, enough about that. How was your meeting?" she said as she took his hand.

"It was great ... I mean there were lots of discussion about hot topics ... mostly related to laparoscopy, and numerous displays with the latest O.R. laparoscopic equipment.

But, my old professor, Mike DeLuca, was right: you come to these meetings to learn, but it's rare that anything **really new** is presented. Mostly it's just a rehash of what's already in the surgical journals.

Sarah, I ran into some people from my training program ... they'd like us to join them for drinks and possibly dinner tonight. I told them that I had to check with you first."

"Well ... I did have plans for the **two** of us. But since they're friends of yours, I don't see why we can't at least meet them for drinks and **pupus**." She was pleased that he had been so considerate and asked her first.

"**Pupus?**

And just when did you start speaking Hawaiian?"

She held up a brochure that she had been reading, and a copy of the American-Hawaiian dictionary that she had found.

"I'm glad you don't mind meeting with some of my old friends. I had to put up with them parading their girlfriends and wives around at our social affairs as a resident.

Now I can show you off!

What have you decided about this afternoon?"

"I'd really like to see Pearl Harbor and the Arizona Memorial. I promised my uncle who was here during the war that we would throw a wreath into the water in memory of his old comrades.

And then I'd like to catch the sunset on the North shore ... if we have time. I hear it's beautiful."

He stood and pulled her close.

"For you, anything. We'll make their plans fit into ours. Let me just track them down, and then we'll be on our way."

*   *   *   *

The business section of downtown Honolulu, this city with such an ominous history, was now difficult to distinguish from most large mainland cities.

They drove onto the Lunalilo Freeway toward Pearl City ... past Honolulu International Airport, Hickam Air Force Base and onto the Kam Highway.

Just past the Pearl Harbor Naval Station was the entrance to the Arizona Memorial. Prior to being shuttled to the Memorial situated in the harbor adjacent to Ford Island, Sarah and Dave were routed into a small theater where they were shown a film about the history of the *Arizona*, from her building and launching ... until she arrived at her final resting place at the harbor's bottom. Eerily lit scenes of the hull of the sunken ship, taken by Navy frogmen with underwater cameras, show *Arizona* as she looks today, stripped of her glory ... the tomb of over a thousand sailors who lost their lives that morning when she had been blown into history.

Authentic Navy launches, manned by active duty sailors, ferried them the short distance across the harbor to the decks of the memorial that straddles the once proud ship. Only the rusted gun turrets remain visible above the water level. The guns had proven useless the morning of the Japanese raid. The crew, arising just before eight a.m., had barely swung into action when the boat was sunk by a bomb down her main smoke stack that ignited her ammunition stores.

For *Arizona* and her crew, the war was over before it had scarcely begun.

They stood at the railing for a few moments, taking in the sights and sounds and smells of the harbor, trying to envision in their mind's eye the historical events that had occurred here.

"You know, you hear and you read about events and places in history, but it's never quite real until you experience it first hand."

She squeezed his hand.

"Now I see why my uncle got so emotional whenever he talked about this place. Several of his old Navy buddies from training days were on *Arizona* and are entombed here."

Following an old Navy tradition, she threw a wreath into the water as the pair stood in silence for a few additional minutes. The launch then returned them to the memorial entrance.

It was almost four o'clock, and the North Shore sunset would have to wait for another day. Dave turned on the radio and found a station playing authentic Hawaiian music.

"Did you know that the Hawaiians were great musicians and composers? In the days of the monarchy, the royal family wrote some of the best known pieces still heard today."

"I am really impressed that you know so much about the Hawaiian people." She nuzzled against his shoulder as he drove.

"I told you it's been a favorite hobby of mine for a long time."

*　　*　　*　　*

Once back in their hotel room, Sarah once again disappeared into the bathroom, only to appear moments later clad in nothing but a towel.

"You showed me a great time today ... now it's my turn to show you one. I think we have time"

She lay down on the bed, discarding the towel as she did.

"We'll make time" was his reply as he quickly undressed and lay down next to her. Passions had been building all day at the harbor. He gently cupped her breast mounds. Then as his hands slowly made their way down to her softer female parts, he teased her nipples with his wet lips.

She guided him into her as their passions intensified to climax level. Now he mounted her and she took all of him in. She held him until the crescendo was complete and their bodies spent.

They lay clinging to one another. The two halves were now whole. Nothing else in the world mattered at that moment.

"I love you, Sarah."

Her immediate reply validated his feelings.

"Oh, Dave. I thought I'd never hear you say those words. I love you too!"

After only a short while the silence was broken. She suddenly sat up and told him about her findings in the brochures.

"I'd like for us to take a few days when your meeting is over and fly to Maui. There's this cute little town called **Hana** that I'd like to visit. It's at the eastern end of the island and it's supposed to be quaint like the Hawaii of old."

He thought to himself that their lovemaking session was being terminated rather abruptly, but he loved her enthusiasm and wasn't about to spoil the moment by not sharing it with her.

"Sounds good to me. Anything you'd like to do is great. Now, how about joining my friends for that drink we promised them, and then we'll find a cozy place for dinner?"

She kissed him one last time.

"Perfect."

She smiled to herself as she arose to get dressed. There were a few more details to her plan that she would work on tomorrow while he was at his meeting.

*　　*　　*　　*

Midsouth—August, 2005

Jack had been busy reviewing the studies provided him by radiology. He was already coming to the conclusion that something appeared to be amiss. The names Li, Hauser, Bledsoe and Fortner seemed to be associated on a disproportionate number of studies. And a number of reports were inconclusive about the presence or absence of stones in the gallbladder and/or common bile duct. The number of ERCP's being performed was also out of proportion based on the relatively few abnormal common bile ducts noted in the studies. He thought it odd that few MRCP's had been ordered, since most gastroenterologists were generally ordering the test prior to performing an ERCP.

He also made note of the fact that Russ Callahan's and Mike Herman's names seemed to appear more often than they should, considering the numbers of physicians in their respective departments.

Jack had an old friend in town at Evansville State University who was a statistician. He planned to ask his help in analyzing the data he was collecting before deciding whether it was worthy of taking to the Executive Committee. He needed to establish a clear correlation with the pathology reports and so would need to talk to Mike Herman as soon as possible.

He just needed a break in his busy office routine and emergency room problems in order to have the time to accomplish things in a timely way.

Chapter 15

▼

Midsouth—2005

Subtle signs are there ... *if* we choose to look for them. Often, we do look but we do not see the truth ... or seeing it, we choose to ignore it.

Marriage is an institution built on mutual trust ... trust that is but a broken promise away. Men are usually assumed to be the guilty party in unfaithful marriages, and seeking sex the main motive; but men sometimes are the victims of inattentive spouses and just seek companionship from another female. Being weak and frequently lonely creatures, men easily fall prey to women who perceive them as vulnerable.

*　　*　　*　　*

Midsouth—Spring 2003

It had started several years earlier when Maggie became so entangled with the affairs of the hospital volunteer services that her home life with Bill began to suffer. This man who had just lost one partner through death was now losing his new spouse to a position that he had helped create.

Maggie was working hard to be a good wife. As the spouse of the CEO of Midsouth, she felt it necessary to increase her visibility at the medical center. But that had only made it more difficult for her to decline requests for help from her and her organization. She was caught in a predicament ... promising him she would slow down, but at the same time wanting her husband to be proud of her.

Alone at home far more than he preferred, Bill had become lonely and depressed.

He created new diversions to keep him apart from the solitude of their home. He announced a new "administrative availability" policy to the hospital employees. In order for after hours workers to have access to him, he often stayed late into the evening and made rounds of the various hospital areas, especially the critical care wards, to assure his accessibility to those people least able to come to him.

* * * *

She was young and vibrant and attractive ... and quickly aroused his passion with her flirtatious advances. She provided him the attention that he was so desperately seeking. Harmless meetings at the hospital soon gave way to secret liaisons apart from the institution. And Maggie, still busy with her volunteer affairs, didn't notice ... or chose to ignore the signs.

When finally she began to curb her hospital work, Bill decided that it was the long-term relationship with his wife that he preferred, and sought to break off the short-lived affair.

The relationship had ended amicably ... or so it seemed.

But little could this lonely man anticipate the pain and suffering in store for his brief indiscretion.

* * * *

Midsouth—September 2005

Jack had many things on his mind. As the years passed, he was becoming more troubled with the direction of medicine. The new generation of doctors was hardly "professional" by his generation's standards. They dressed casually, worked bankers hours, and participated in after-hour "on-call" pools that often had them taking call only once every several weeks. Patients were relegated to "pot-luck" when seeking medical help apart from routine business hours.

And now this Fortner thing. Was there any thing to it ... and if so, who was the leader and what was the motive?

When would he find the time to ferret out the facts?

Just as he was hoping that the E.R. would remain quiet on his call day, his beeper went off. It was the emergency department's number.

"Damn, I hope that it's nothing real urgent."

"Hi, June. It's Dr. Davidson", he said to the E.R. secretary.

"Dr. Li needs to talk to you right away. Please hold." More anxious moments followed as he waited for Frank Li's voice.

"Jack, I'm afraid it's going to be a bad day for you on call. I've got two people in a shootout from our favorite neighboring county, Rockland. One probably has an arterial injury to his leg. I've ordered an arteriogram on him. The other has chest and abdominal wounds. I've already placed a chest tube; he appears stable for the moment. We've got the usual lab work cooking, and I've given each one some antibiotics. Anything else you need?"

"How about a Valium?" quipped Jack.

"No, Frank. My, they're sure starting early today.

It sounds like you've got things under control as usual. Just make sure some blood is available. I'll be there in about ten minutes.

Better let the O.R. and anesthesia know what to expect."

"They're typed and cross-matched for four units each and anesthesia is already on their way down. The O.R. is readying a room", said Frank.

Jack hung up the phone and quickly called the office. They were used to these sudden changes in daily plans and took it in stride.

For Jack it was going to be "just another one of those days."

✻   ✻   ✻   ✻

He had been right about the day. The gunshot wound victims kept him in the O.R. until late afternoon. While the patient with the leg injury underwent arteriography, he took the more seriously injured of the two directly to the operating room when the patient became unstable. Jack knew that the best place for such an individual was in the O.R. where he and his anesthesia colleagues could control things best.

The chest tube inserted by Frank Li had controlled the chest wound adequately; the drainage had slowed down to a trickle indicating no major vessel injury. So at least he didn't have to concern himself with two major areas.

One of the other bullets, however, had passed through the right lobe of the liver, the patient's large intestine, multiple loops of small intestine and a large mesenteric vessel ... before exiting the body. This required some quick suturing to control the vascular injury. Jack had one assistant hold pressure on the liver wound until he could place some blunt sutures to control the bleeding there.

Then he repaired the small bowel holes with suture, removed a badly damaged segment of large intestine and left the patient with a colostomy to protect the abdominal cavity from further contamination by spilled intestinal contents.

The operation had taken about three hours. While he was working, Russ Callahan had called into the O.R. to let him know that the other patient did have an arterial injury to the proximal femoral artery. So as quickly as he could dispatch the first patient's postoperative paperwork, he was back in the E.R. preparing the second patient for surgery.

It was almost mid-afternoon, and he hadn't made it to the office at all ... and wouldn't this day. The girls at the office had taken care of rescheduling things. He would do the second gunshot wound patient and follow that with a scheduled hernia repair ... the poor individual had been waiting since mid-morning in the outpatient unit.

Fortunately, the femoral artery injury was easily accessible. However, the damage was fairly extensive, requiring an interposition graft of the large saphenous vein taken from the patient's opposite leg. Once he had sewn the vein in place and removed the clamps that controlled blood flow to the injured vessel, blood again flowed into the lower limb and foot. Jack could feel the patient's pulse on the top of the foot and hear the sounds of the blood flowing with a special instrument called a Doppler.

The first patient had been taken to the I.C.U. while Jack did the vascular repair, and the second patient would go there after a brief stay in the Post Anesthesia Care Unit.

He followed with the hernia repair, finally finishing at a few minutes after five p.m. It was nearly five-thirty by the time he took care of the usual post-op dictation, paper work and had talked to the patients' families.

Then he headed to the I.C.U. to check on the status of the two critical patients. Sharon and Elaine were both still on duty, and reported to him that everything was stable with both patients. They brought him a cup of coffee when they saw him enter.

"Why don't you come and have a seat in our lounge, Dr. Davidson? You must be tired and hungry after such a long day." Elaine found a piece of cake to go with his coffee.

"I was actually just on my way to the office when the E.R. introduced me to the two newest members of the 'knife and gun club'" ... referring to the two gunshot victims.

"I guess I'll see you two in the morning if I don't get sidetracked again. Tell your replacements this evening that I'll be stopping back a little later to check on things, but call me if there are any significant changes or abnormal lab work."

Since it was after normal working hours and the non-clinical areas of the hospital were virtually deserted except for a few maintenance people, Jack decided to do a little snooping in medical records on the Fortner matter.

As he passed the Pathology Department en route to medical records, the door suddenly flung open emitting Mike Herman. Each was surprised to see the other.

"Mike, what's a nine-to-fiver like you doing here at this hour?" said Jack. Most pathologists kept fairly regular hours. It was now going on seven o'clock.

"Jack! I might ask the same about you. I've just been working on some things for the Special Hematology Lab."

He was uncharacteristically brusque and excused himself, saying he had to get home. Jack thought his behavior a little strange, but brushed it off and continued on to medical records.

* * * *

Jack carried a copy of the list of patients that Danielle Morgan had given him, just in case he found himself in the hospital with spare time to work on the review.

Being Chief of Surgery, the night clerk in medical records knew him on sight and didn't hesitate to fulfill his request for charts, even though the list was lengthy. He was tired after his full day in surgery, but sat down and began a methodical review. He hoped to find enough facts to further substantiate the information he had already obtained.

He brought a legal pad on which to tabulate the data. He had constructed columns with headings to help organize the findings. The main items he wanted to review were:

1. Any E.R. visits for complaints referable to gallbladder disease

2. The chief complaint when the patient presented for surgery

3. Supplemental radiology reports, both inpatient and outpatient (where possible)

4. Operative reports referable to the gallbladder/biliary tree

5. The physicians involved in the care of the patient, including E.R., surgeon, pathologist, radiologist, and any other consultants, and the primary care physician

6. Any other miscellaneous and interesting facts that he might find.

Jack was getting sleepy as he sifted through the charts. Staring at the three-foot high stack of charts still needing his scrutiny, he knew he should get some rest just in case the E.R. called him again before morning. But he was committed to getting the task done ... especially now that he had a personal interest in seeing what relationship, if any, existed.

After reviewing about twenty charts and extracting the information for his lists, he suddenly realized that a pattern was developing: at least a third of the patients were seen by the same E.R. physician for vague abdominal complaints, sent to the same family physician or internist, frequently had pre-operative ERCP and *all* were then operated on by Dave Fortner for gallbladder related problems.

Many of the initial gallbladder ultrasound reports indicated no stones were seen. Yet the admission history and physical indicated that stones were reported seen in the gallbladder on the ultrasound exam. He would have to determine if another study had been done elsewhere and that could take time.

Suddenly, he was wide-awake again. He continued his tabulation and thirty more charts revealed similar data. Now he was almost certain that he was on to something important, some type of medical fraud and conspiracy happening right here, right now at Midsouth.

And right under everyone's noses ... his own colleagues perpetrating something that he didn't fully comprehend. What was their motive: money? power?

And who was involved?

Sitting alone in the medical record department at night, a shiver suddenly went up his spine. The hour was late and the lighting dim ... adding to the dread that he was suddenly feeling.

At that very moment, he was taken aback by footsteps that seemed to be coming his way. Was it just a mind trick?

No! The steps were real and definitely coming toward him. His mind was suddenly flooded with thoughts of horror movies where someone invariably gets murdered in a scene similar to this.

But a janitor emptying waste cans walked on by, allaying his fears ... much to his relief. He decided that he had had enough excitement for one day. After collecting up his personal things, he asked the clerk to hold the remaining charts. He would try to return the following day and complete that portion of his review.

After a quick stop in the I.C.U., where everything was stable, he continued on home.

Lynn was in bed, awake and waiting for him. He quickly summarized what he had discovered during his chart review, and his new found fears.

She confessed that the whole thing was becoming very unnerving to her, and thought that it should be to him as well.

"I don't mind saying that I was a bit frightened sitting there alone in medical records. But I feel better now that I'm home here with you."

"What a sweet thing to say." She kissed him deeply and let him know that she would be pleased with more intimate affection.

CHAPTER 16
▼

Evansville, N.C.—October 2004

Mike was delighted. The timing couldn't have been more perfect. It had been far too long since their lake meeting. While he had been searching for the time and opportunity to take her out ... and to show her off, the lab had kept him too busy. He had thought about her almost daily; yet somehow he had failed to even call her.

"Danielle, it's Mike Herman. How are you?"

"Well. Mike, it's great to hear from you." She hesitated briefly.

"After our day at the lake, I thought I would have heard from you sooner. I was beginning to think that you had forgotten me."

He explained the many things that had been going on with the hematology lab, and why he hadn't called.

"But I know that's not much of an excuse," he added as an apology.

She accepted his explanation without reservation.

Then, in typical female fashion, she continued rambling ... so he just sat and listened. He took this as a good sign in their relationship ... being forgiving and being personal.

"But I'm talking too much about me. How have you been?"

"I've been fine. As I explained about the lab, it just takes up all my time. I've been to Chicago three times ... and I just got back from New York a few days ago. It doesn't leave me much time for socializing.

But it hasn't kept me from thinking about you. And I'm really sorry I didn't take the time to call and explain that to you before now."

She was pleased that he had added that.

"So I'd like to make it up to you now.

Dr. Jack Davidson and his wife have invited me to a cocktail party at their home two weeks from next Saturday night. They suggested I bring a date.

So if you're free, I'd love to have you come with me?"

She feigned having to check her social calendar.

"My calendar is all clear that night. I'd love to go with you, Mike"

"Great. I'll plan to pick you up around seven-thirty. But I hope that we can have lunch or at least coffee before then.

I'll try to call you ... but if I don't, assume that I'm busy with my work but still thinking of you."

"That's so sweet of you, Mike. You know where I work. So I'll look forward to your call."

She oozed femininity even over the phone. Her goodbye was amazingly sensual. Mike felt a twinge of sexual arousal again as he hung up the phone.

At home that evening, Danielle turned to **Gizmo**.

"I think we have him right where we want him, my little furry friend."

Gizmo purred in response.

*   *   *   *

"He just called and invited me to a party at Dr. Davidson's home."

"Well, this time you'd better not screw it up. We'll be ready for him at your place, so you know what to do.

You know, he is kind of cute, so I know you'll have a good time with him while accomplishing business."

Danielle blushed at the thought, and told *sister* that this time she would unequivocally deliver on her promise.

*   *   *   *

Jack and Lynn Davidson didn't consider themselves part of the social elite of Evansville, but they felt the occasional need to entertain friends and colleagues as a form of repayment for their support of his business.

Like most of his colleagues, Jack viewed medical administration people with extreme caution. However, he had now known Bill Smithson for most of his tenure at Midsouth, and had generally regarded him as friendly and trustworthy. Being an M.D. as well, made him more like one of the group. He also liked Maggie. Her presence in the hospital as Chief of Volunteer Services made her a most admired citizen of the medical complex.

So the couple had been included on the invitation list.

Jack also liked to invite people he worked with at the hospital but didn't necessarily know socially. He had met Mike Herman shortly after his arrival in Evansville, and had even served on several committees with him. Other than that minimal association, he didn't really know him at all ... but he seemed like a very nice person.

So Jack thought this would be an excellent opportunity to foster the relationship and get to know him better. He encouraged him to bring a date.

* * * *

An opportunity to get together before the party never materialized ... Mike had gone out of town again on business. But he remembered lessons learned growing up in a household full of women.

He had called Danielle and reconfirmed their date. And he had called Lynn Davidson and asked her help. He didn't know what to tell Danielle about the dress code for the evening. So Lynn had been kind enough to call Danielle.

Danielle in turn had confirmed that to Mike, and thanked him for such thoughtfulness. She couldn't remember anyone ever taking such time for her in the past.

She looked forward to the evening, and her chance to prove herself to *sister*.

* * * *

Evansville, N.C.—November 20, 2004

The big night had finally arrived, and Mike was a few minutes late arriving at Danielle's house. The hematology lab projects continued to be all time-consuming, even on weekends.

He was as nervous as he could ever remember being before a date.

And Danielle was equally anxious. She sat watching the street for his car. When he finally arrived, she opened the door almost before he had a chance to ring the doorbell. The pair stood staring at each other like two love struck teenagers until she finally invited him in. Her silhouette in the doorway had totally captivated him.

"You look gorgeous!" he blurted out.

She blushed and then responded with a light kiss on the lips.

"I'm so glad that you invited me to the Davidson's tonight. They're such nice people. I've been looking forward to this since you called. I'm really sorry we weren't able to get together before tonight, but I understand your busy schedule."

"But we have tonight. So let's not stand here talking about my work. Let's just concentrate on you and me getting to know each other better.

Are you ready to go?"

"I just need to get my jacket since it's quite cool in the evenings now.

I feel like Cinderella going to the ball ... one doesn't get many opportunities to dress up in Evansville."

She wore a silver and black beaded cocktail dress with a modestly plunging bodice that uncovered enough of her breasts to make any man dream of how they must look fully exposed. And that would make him the envy of the other men at the party ... a feeling that men thoroughly enjoy.

"Ready when you are" she said as she returned with her *faux fur* jacket that complemented her dress nicely.

"And may I say that you look especially handsome tonight." She reached out to straighten his tie.

Now it was Mike's turn to blush ... he wasn't accustomed to flattery and never thought of himself as "handsome".

"Thank you" he responded.

He escorted her to the car, his hand round her waist. After helping her get situated, including fastening her seat belt, he closed her door and went to the driver's side.

"You know, I'm really looking forward to seeing the Davidson home. I hear it's a real show place. And I'm looking forward to meeting Lynn Davidson. She was so kind to help a stranger like me out with this dress code business."

"It was really kind of you to arrange for her to call me", Danielle said with a coquettish tone.

"You're very unusual for a bachelor ... so very thoughtful."

"With a mother and three sisters at home, I've had lots of training. They told me how inconsiderate most men are and convinced me that women deserve more respect.

I guess their persistence paid off."

They were nearing the Davidson house.

The driveway approach to the home was reminiscent of the avenue of oaks from *Gone With The Wind*. The house was a two story Georgian mansion situated strategically at the end of the oak lined driveway with selected trees illuminated with spotlights placed near their bases.

Jack and Lynn were positioned near the door, ready to greet each guest as they arrived.

"A nice touch" thought Mike. His parents did the same at the restaurant any time they were there.

"Mike, I'm so glad you could come", said Jack as they shook hands.

"And this is Danielle Morgan" Mike quickly added, turning toward her.

"And this is Lynn" Jack said turning to his wife.

"Welcome to you both.

It's so nice to finally meet you Mike. Jack and I met Danielle before at a hospital outing; it's so wonderful that the two of you could come to our home."

"She's lovely isn't she?" Lynn whispered to Mike as Danielle was being introduced to other guests.

He nodded his approval.

"Well, let's get you both something to drink. After the guests all arrive, I want to show you our home."

The couple took champagne filled flutes, plates of finger food and moved into the den with the other guests. Russ and Bobbi Callahan moved toward them.

"Danielle, it's nice to see you out of the department. And Mike, it's good to see you too. Have you two been dating long?"

"Actually, it's our first formal date." He explained how they had met at the lake.

"It's so nice of Jack and Lynn to have this party. Their home is beautiful," offered Bobbi.

"Lynn is going to give us a tour when she can" replied Danielle.

"You'll really love their things."

Russ and Bobbi excused themselves, heading for Bill and Maggie Smithson, who had just arrived. Mike and Danielle were left alone momentarily. They took the liberty to remove themselves to a vacant corner, but Lynn quickly spied them and made her way to the couple, not wanting them to feel neglected.

"Come on and let me show you the house. I think most of our guests are here now. Jack's going to join us momentarily ... if he can break away."

She began the tour in the living room. Besides the exquisite colors of the walls, there were countless original paintings and signed prints representing well-known major artists and prominent local artists as well. An antique grand piano sat parallel to one wall.

"It belonged to Jack's uncle. It's about a hundred years old and still plays beautifully."

Lynn sat down at the keyboard and illustrated its tone.

Jack intervened and asked to borrow Mike for a few minutes.

"Take your time and introduce him around. Danielle and I will just sit here and get better acquainted until you get back."

Danielle recounted to Lynn her brief relationship with Mike and how they had met. After only a few minutes, Jack returned with Mike. The four continued the tour, quickly moving upstairs and ending in the downstairs study, Jack's favorite room.

The library or study of the Davidson home was their refuge from the outside world. Jack and Lynn had renovated it several times; the final and current version was truly a masterpiece of design and color.

Pocket doors allowed the complete exclusion of the room from the rest of the house and the outside world … if so desired. The wall that housed the pocket doors had built-in bookshelves of dark mahogany stained wood. The opposing three walls were finished in a royal blue above chair rails, with matching color paisley print wallpaper below.

The bookshelves housed an eclectic group of books ranging from Lynn's extensive collection of cookbooks, to recently published volumes of fiction and medical books. They also had a section for volumes related to art glass and paintings.

The pride of Jack's collection, housed in a special glass enclosed casing, were original signed volumes of poetry by Robert Frost and Carl Sandburg.

The opposing walls were filled with original oil paintings by a variety of artists including Buckley Moss and prominent local artists. A four-piece set of authenticated prints by the French artist Jules Cheret adorned the wall above a Jefferson table.

Mike and Danielle were overwhelmed and momentarily speechless.

"I've never seen such a diverse collection of beautiful things in one home before. I love the colors in the room and the way you have things displayed."

"Jack and I did most of the work with the help of a decorator friend."

"Well, maybe you two ought to go into the business," offered Danielle.

"You could turn this place into your own museum."

"Believe me, you're not the first one to tell us that. It's kind of been the standing joke in the family for years that we need one house for our various collectibles, and another to live in."

Mike squeezed Danielle's hand. He thought to himself how nice it must be to have the security of a wife and a home like theirs. But he wasn't ready to share that thought with anyone ... especially Danielle. At least not yet.

"You two need a refill", Lynn said, as she suddenly noticed them standing there with empty glasses.

"I'll only be a minute." She returned with full glasses.

"Jack, I just want to show Danielle my quilt collection, and then I think they will probably have seen all they want to see."

They went into the solarium where Lynn kept a large armoire filled with her creations. She took several out to show Danielle.

It had been a wonderful evening. Mike suddenly looked at his watch and realized that almost two hours had gone by, and that many of the guests had already left. He took that as his cue to collect up Danielle and prepare to do the same.

He was anxious to be alone with her. He had been observing her all evening and finding her more exquisite and exciting with each glance. Mike took her hand as she returned with Lynn and led her toward the entrance foyer.

Her mind was filled of thoughts of what might lie beyond the door of the Davidson home. This was the big night that she had promised herself would prove her loyalty and devotion to **sister** once and for all.

And if she had a little fun in the pursuit of that goal ... well so much the better for them both!

"We've had a wonderful evening" Mike said. "But I think it's time for us to go."

Dave Fortner and his fiancée, Sarah Coleman, approached the door at the same time.

Dave extended his hand to Mike.

"I'm sorry we didn't get a chance to talk at all.

I don't think you've met Sarah?"

"Not formally.

I've seen you at the hospital. It's nice to finally meet you.

And this is Danielle Morgan. I don't know if you know each other."

"I've had her help me in the x-ray department on occasion.

Have you and Sarah met?"

"No, I don't think so" each answered, almost in unison.

They shook hands.

Dave and Sarah left.

"Well, thanks for showing us your beautiful home. We just loved it", added Danielle.

"Don't be strangers", said Lynn. She gave each of them a hug. Jack and Mike exchanged handshakes.

Outside in the shadow of the trees leading to the car, Mike pulled Danielle to himself and kissed her passionately. There was no resistance on her part.

"I've wanted you to do that all evening", she said. They kissed again while getting into the car.

"Let's go back to my place." He felt strangely warm all the way to her house. Barely inside the door, they reached for each other like hungry animals that suddenly had found their prey.

She led him into the bedroom. Now he helped her out of her dress and at long last saw exposed those heaving breasts that had held his attention all evening. She pulled his shirt off and helped him remove his trousers and underwear. He stood there naked, unable to hide his erection.

She placed her hand there as they lay down on the bed. She wasted no time inviting him to penetrate her.

As he entered her repeatedly, his hand found her breast and his mouth her soft lips. Again and again their bodies met, until spent they lay together in unspoken fulfillment.

Mike was exhausted. After a short while, Danielle turned and whispered:

"Why don't you spend the night? You were wonderful ... *we* were wonderful together."

He wasn't sure how to respond. This man of thirty-something years had suddenly experienced his first intimacy. It was new to him while she had been married before. He wasn't sure of his obligations under the circumstances.

"I think I had better go home and get some sleep. I didn't mention it, but I have an early morning meeting tomorrow, even though it's Sunday, and then I have to catch a flight to Boston ... more business, you know.

Besides, what would people think if they saw me coming out of your house in the morning?"

"Well, I'm not sure if I care what my neighbors think." She nuzzled against his bare chest as she uttered the words.

"But I understand. Will you call me tomorrow before you leave?"

"Of course."

They lingered for a few more minutes exchanging kisses, and then slowly disengaged from one another.

She watched him as he dressed, then followed him to the door.

One last kiss and he was gone. Mike still wasn't sure how to handle this situation so new to him. Although he loved the feeling, he was unsure of how to proceed.

She lay back down on the bed.

The phone rang.

"Danielle, I'm so proud of you. We didn't quite get everything we needed, but it's not your fault. We had a little technical problem. You'll need to arrange another session just in case."

"Thank you, **Sister**. I'm sure I can arrange that.

And you were right ... I did have fun!"

CHAPTER 17

▼

Oahu, Hawaii—April 2004

The *Kahunas*, the wise ones, say that Maui was formed five million years ago, the result of undersea volcanic eruptions. Two adjacent volcanoes were formed, eventually merging to form one island: Maui. One is represented by the west Maui Mountains; the other, Mt. Haleakala, rises majestically to an altitude of 10,023 feet above sea level. Now dormant, the volcanoes once spewed molten magma down their slopes. Gradual erosion led to the formation of the modern central plains, home to the main city, Kahalui.

The first known migrants to Maui were the Marquesas, who arrived about 750 A.D., after observing that migrant birds returning from the general direction of what proved to be the Hawaiian Islands were always fat. They sent their best explorers and hunters to settle the islands. The Tahitians, from neighboring islands in the Polynesian chain, followed them after several centuries. They introduced their gods and goddesses and their religion, including their strict social system, or *kapu*. The latter affected all aspects of life and formed the core of the ancient Hawaiian culture.

Life in Maui and the neighboring Hawaiian islands remained relatively simple until the mid-1700's when King Kamehameha took up residence in Lahaina after conquering Maui. Things further changed when Captain James Cook discovered the Hawaiian (Sandwich) Islands in November 1778. His discovery brought whalers, traders, and missionaries who would usher Hawaii into the modern era. The monarchy would continue until 1893 when Queen Liliukalani was forced to relinquish control. The following year, the Republic of Hawaii was formed, and in 1898 the islands were annexed by the United States. Hawaii became an official U.S. territory in 1900 and the fiftieth state in 1959.

* * * *

Waialae Coast, Maui—April 2004

Their week on Oahu was nearing an end. The surgical meeting had concluded and Sarah and Dave spent the last few free afternoons doing tourist things. And in between, they engaged in passionate lovemaking.

They caught the short flight from Honolulu to Kahalui, on Maui, where they planned an additional four-day stay along the Waialae Coast. The location gave them ready access to all the sights of the island.

Four more days in paradise before reality would once again slap them in the face and force them to return to Evansville and Midsouth.

For now, they just wanted to sit on the sandy beach, listen to the sounds of the rolling surf, and wonder if the incoming tide would engulf their blanket and force them to move higher up onto the dune.

* * * *

On their first full day on Maui, they drove to Lahaina, the former whaling capital of the Pacific. In the years following World War II, as the Hawaiian Islands were "discovered" by tourists, it had been transformed into a tourist haven much like Honolulu and Oahu, only on a lesser scale.

The 1990's saw an influx of chain type establishments into even the smaller Hawaiian towns and villages. The couple was surprised to find a **Hard Rock Café** incongruously situated on Lahaina's main street amidst souvenir shops and trendy boutiques.

The following day they drove to the summit of Mt. Haleakala, the eastern volcanic peak that had helped form the island. From the summit, Hawaii and Molokai and several smaller islands can be seen. Because the summit surface has the appearance of lunar terrain, it was used for training by the Apollo astronauts before the 1969 moon landing.

With her plans set and only two days to go, Sarah suggested that they go to Hana the following morning and that they take a picnic lunch and some wine since the driving time in each direction was several hours despite the relatively short distance.

Nestled at the eastern end of Maui, **Hana** is a vestige of the Hawaii of old. Previously accessible only by water or air, it has been connected to the rest of the island by road since 1927.

The drive from Kahalui to Hana requires a grueling two hour drive by car despite the meager fifty-mile distance. The trek there follows the rugged coastline with its more than six hundred twists and turns. Streams emanating from the slopes of Haleakala frequently erode portions of the road. The **mauka,** or mountain view contains abundant waterfalls cascading into lush streams amidst exotic fragrant foliage; the **makai,** or ocean view features the unending deep blue waters of the Pacific.

Hana is home to the **taro** plant, the root used to make **poi,** the staple of the Hawaiian diet of old. And here, near this remote ancient village, Sarah's plan would be launched.

This was their last full day in Hawaii and they intended to make the most of it. Their flight home would leave late the following afternoon.

The road from the Waialae coast area took them through the outskirts of Kahalui, past the airport, and then along the northern fringes of Haleakala.

"*767*", Dave remarked as a jumbo jet passed overhead. Sarah acknowledged his remark, but didn't have a clue how to tell one aircraft from the other.

"Those things have a takeoff weight of over a half million pounds when fully loaded and headed for the mainland."

"You just know everything about flying and airplanes, don't you?" she cooed, as she snuggled next to him and took his right arm in hers. Keeping him pleased was important considering the matters that lay ahead.

Kahalui and the airport quickly faded into the distance as they progressed along the Hana highway. The road began to narrow as they passed by the last of several small villages and the final vestiges of the slopes of Haleakala.

Fog and clouds drifted down from the summit, intermittently obscuring their view. Periods of intense sunshine were interspersed with virtual darkness.

"I'm going to put the top up and the lights on ... before we get soaked from the spray. And with these narrow roads in this dim light ... I want to make sure cars coming toward us can see us."

Soon the road was an undulating mass of asphalt, twisting and turning from coastal overhang to inland recess. Single lane bridges punctuated their way, necessitating their yielding to oncoming traffic more than once. Road signs pointed out the many nature stops: hiking trails, waterfalls, natural flora, and bird sanctuaries. They stopped to enjoy several en route ... but Sarah was more interested in getting to their destination and the beaches beyond.

Fifty long miles of twists and turns made them feel like they had just survived an amusement park ride. But the scenery had been breathtaking ... especially the unencumbered views of the Pacific from shoreline to infinity.

And the fog and spray had continued their cat and mouse game throughout the sojourn ... ever present, ever fleeting ... at times giving an eerie glow as they passed the dense interior forests.

Finally, Dave pointed to the sign ahead.

"Welcome to **Hana**."

"Perfect", thought Sarah to herself.

The town was small, consisting of the authentic nineteenth century Hasagawa general store and gas station, the Hana hotel, artist shops, a gas station and several restaurants.

It was already early afternoon when they stopped for lunch at the Hana hotel's restaurant that featured a beautiful *lanai*. Sarah was in no hurry. She purposefully spent the next several hours browsing the various shops, buying and addressing post cards to people back in Evansville.

She had studied the maps of the area while in Honolulu, and knew that the road past town led to the Seven Pools at O'heo Gulch, caves and the remote beaches at Lelekea Bay. The sun was waning towards the west as they arrived at the secluded beach area.

"Oh Dave, it's perfect."

"You know, Sarah, we really should hurry along if we're going to get back before dark. I mean, that road is a monster in the best of light."

"I've got an idea ... why don't we just spend the night here instead of driving all the way back to the hotel? It's already late afternoon. We've got enough food and drinks in the picnic basket for tonight, and we can catch breakfast back in Hana in the morning.

It's our last day here and I can't think of anything I'd rather do than just be alone here with you on this secluded beach.

I assure you, I will make it worth your while."

He needed no more coaxing than that. What else could a man ask for ... alone on a secluded beach in Hawaii with a beautiful woman that he was now certain that he was in love with?

Yes. They would spend this last night on the beach outside *Hana*. It would be their *secret* place.

*   *   *   *

Hana, Hawaii—April 2004

Their last night in the islands was spent amidst the backdrop of a full tropical moon illuminating the glimmering shores of the remote deserted beach they had found.

Sarah had excused herself while Dave unloaded the towels and blankets and food from the car. When she reemerged, she was totally naked.

"I promised you that the night here would be worthwhile. So do what you will with me."

He had never had such an open invitation to lust in his life. Here she stood in all her naked glory, inviting him to take her. He quickly stripped off his clothes and joined her on the sand. Hand in hand they walked into the water; they eased into the surf while fondling one another and sharing a deep passionate kiss.

"You know, this kind of reminds me of that scene from the movie *From Here To Eternity*, where the couple is rolling in the sand, madly kissing one another ... except that we're naked and they looked like they should have been."

Dave couldn't believe his good fortune ... being here with such a gorgeous and sensuous woman ... him ... a man who had never been able to make it with women, let alone a beauty queen.

He stood in the surf kissing and fondling her voluptuous breasts and erect nipples. They emerged from the cool Pacific water and lay down on the blanket where he made love to her, again and again.

There was no tomorrow ... no return to Evansville ... no Midsouth ... just *Sarah*.

The night slowly gave way to dawn, their time spent in alternating bouts of lovemaking and slumber in the company of each other's arms.

"Sarah, did you just hear some noises from behind the sand dunes? It almost sounded like someone talking and laughing."

Several times she disappeared behind the dunes and emerged to tell him that there was no one there. Sarah caressed him and assured him that it was just the *menehune*, the little people of Hawaiian lore. Their secret place and their secret affair remained safely hidden from the world.

He laughed at her use of the Hawaiian folklore tale and gleefully agreed that it must be the explanation.

Dawn's rosy fingers soon announced the sun's imminent arrival ... the first light of a new day and the impending close of their time in Hana and the Hawaiian islands.

"Let's stop at Hasagawa's and get a few things before we get back on that long, windy road" she whispered as she grabbed him and rolled him over on the blanket.

"One more time, my love, and then I'm afraid it's time to return to reality."

She took him in one last time ... forcefully, fully, until both were wholly spent.

"Dave Fortner, did I tell you that I love you?"

"Only four hundred times. But I can stand to hear number four hundred and one."

They laughed as she whispered it one last time. He nibbled at her ear, kissed her neck and mouth, and then stood.

"I guess if we're going to Hana for breakfast, we'd better put some clothes on."

She once more disappeared behind the dunes, excusing herself as she went.

"Girl things, I guess."

He didn't notice a van parked along the beach in the distance.

She reemerged and got into the car as he placed the last items in the back. They stopped briefly in Hana for breakfast as planned and then entered the serpentine portion of the road back to Kahalui. She fell asleep only to awaken to the sound of an airplane passing overhead.

"We'll be at the hotel shortly." She kissed him and fell back asleep. At the hotel, they made love one last time before Dave fell into exhaustive slumber ... only to be awakened three hours later by the alarm warning them it was time to depart for the airport.

The plane that would shuttle them to the mainland was touching down as they approached the gate. Dave disappeared for a moment, reappearing with a *pikake* lei that he placed around Sarah's neck.

"This is for the most incredible night that I've ever spent in my life.

I'll never forget it," he said.

"I'm sure neither of us will" she said, thanking him for the beautiful flower lei.

He could not imagine just how prophetic those words were.

The long flight home lay ahead. In some ways though, it would be good to get back home and back to the old routine.

CHAPTER 18
▼

Midsouth—Late September 2005

Jack Davidson could be extraordinarily impatient, especially when waiting for others to do things for him. He was used to being in control, and disliked it when things were beyond his control ... like waiting for the radiology reports necessary for his investigation into the allegations of wrongdoing by Dave Fortner.

Danielle had apologized for the delay, but again blamed it on problems with reprogramming their computers. Jack had spoken directly to Russ Callahan about the matter, but he had indicated that his hands were tied by the computer situation too. He would do what he could ... but that had amounted to nothing. The system simply had a speed of its own.

Jack decided to talk to Mike Herman and begin working on the pathology correlation. But that meeting was reminiscent of his meetings with Russ Callahan: professional, a feeling of mild annoyance for having to go out of his way ... and more delay in getting the requested information.

Jack tried to be understanding ... and could have been more so if he felt he were asking for something out of the ordinary. The information he was seeking was routine as far as he knew ... and generally accessible with a few typed entries on the computer keyboard.

He finally decided to force the issue during a subsequent encounter with Mike Herman. He asked him rather pointedly if he thought it possible that a normal pathologic sample could be reported as ***abnormal***.

Jack realized the implication of the question posed.

As did Mike!

"You mean, is there someone in my department capable of falsifying results?

Jack, I'm not sure I like the intent or purpose of the question. But to answer it: yes, of course. But it would be terribly difficult, given the number of people involved in processing a single specimen.

You know, it all starts in your department. Your O.R. people handle it first and then pass it on to us. They are responsible for labeling things correctly before sending it to our department for accession. If a specimen was incorrectly labeled, we wouldn't necessarily know anything about it.

Then the specimen would generally be handled by several people in my department before getting to one of the pathologists for reading.

And then there is the typed report.

You might want to check with Quality Assurance about investigating that.

Jack, I suppose it's possible to falsify reports, but I'd have to say that it's highly improbable that it could be done without being detected.

What makes you ask such a question, anyway?"

"It's just something I'm working on for the hospital ... and it might help to explain some things I've discovered that I don't quite understand.

Of course it would be illegal. I'm reasonably sure no one here would do that."

Jack realized the sensitive and accusatory nature of what he had asked, and just wanted to let it die for the moment.

"Please don't discuss this conversation with anyone ... let's just leave it between you and me."

Mike assured him that it would be their little secret.

Not sure at all about the ramifications of what he had just alleged, Jack left Mike's office and weaved his way out of the Pathology Department.

* * * *

The special phone rang, the one that he alone answered.

"He was just here in the department asking about surgical samples and the possibility of reports being switched or falsified. He's been snooping around radiology as well, reviewing reports on gallbladder testing."

"We're trying to stall him as best we can. But something will have to be done before this goes any further. Frankly, he's beginning to make me more than a little nervous.

But I'm sure that we can arrange a little something to throw him off the track. Relax and leave it to me.

I'll notify the boss."

*   *   *   *

Evansville—October 7, 2005

The Davidsons had scheduled a trip to Boston for the following week to attend the annual clinical congress of one of Jack's surgical societies. It would be good to leave the mounting anxiety of the Fortner affair behind for a short time anyway.

Jack had become tired of the hectic daily office and surgery schedules in recent years. So a meeting or two a year gave him a respite from those ever pressing concerns.

And it was great not to have E.R. call for a while. With an ever-increasing volume of trauma referred to Midsouth in recent years, call presented an increasingly major problem for surgeons in particular. In addition to being time consuming and occurring at all hours of the day and night, it often paid little or nothing, while at the same time placing surgeons at higher risk for malpractice suits and exposure to communicable diseases.

Jack and Lynn's flight arrived at Logan airport right on schedule. They had allowed a few extra days for a side trip to the coastal portions of northern New England.

They passed through Portsmouth, New Hampshire and then took the old coastal Route One through picturesque coastal Maine to their final destination, Bar Harbor. They had visited the area only once before, and had been there just long enough to know that they wanted to return. So this would give them the opportunity to visit adjacent Acadia National Park, the light house at Bass Harbor, browse the many tourist shops and ... of course, dine on scallops and lobster.

The weekend passed too quickly, and soon they were reentering Boston's city limits late on Sunday evening, longing for the comfort of a bed after the long ride back. At the hotel, Jack proceeded to the registration desk where he was handed a message to call his office manager immediately.

His immediate concern was for his family and office staff.

But the news was anything but what he expected.

* * * *

Kevin had finished his hospital rounds early and was walking to the parking lot when he spied Dave Fortner heading toward him.
"I trust you're still enjoying your participation in the *project?*"
"Of course."
Kevin smiled as he fondled the door handle of his new Mercedes.
"We're keeping you busy enough, too, I trust?"
They each smiled at the rhetorical question posed by the other.
"I've got about all I can handle most days."
Dave patted Kevin on the shoulder.
"Just keep up the good work," he offered.
Dave's voice trailed off as he proceeded to his own car.

* * * *

Kevin Bledsoe, M.D., was a fellowship-trained gastroenterologist. And like so many of the physicians at Midsouth, he was a transplant to the area.

He had been stationed at Bishop Air Force base near Evansville and had become aware that Midsouth was recruiting physicians in his specialty about the time he was due to be discharged.

He and his wife Jennifer liked the area immensely, and jumped at the chance to stay there in practice. The first few years in practice validated their choice. Business had been exceptionally good, affording them a life style that neither had been accustomed to growing up in rural Oregon.

Kevin was an avid golfer. Jennifer played tennis with a passion. Appropriately, they had purchased a new home in the country club section of town, where the garage housed a Mercedes-Benz 500SEL for him and a BMW 300 convertible for her.

The couple had been married for eight years when they settled into private practice. They had met at the University of Oregon. While he attended medical school in Portland during their dating years, Jennifer had stayed in Eugene and worked for a software company. They were married the weekend after his graduation from medical school.

By the time he completed his residency and fellowship training, they had two children, now ages eight and six. Jennifer did consulting work in the Portland area until their move to Evansville.

Jennifer had taken up tennis with the other junior officer's wives while Kevin was in the service. She became one of the local stars on base and often participated with other team members in competitions held locally and at other nearby military facilities, often necessitating her staying out overnight.

As his practice quickly grew, time became a more valuable commodity for the couple ... he with the practice, and her with the children and sports activities.

Kevin's specialty was in a state of flux: what had started as a branch of internal medicine that dealt with gastrointestinal and liver disorders, had escalated into an almost totally procedure driven practice similar to surgery.

He was performing an ever increasing number of endoscopic procedures of the upper and lower gastrointestinal tract and bile and pancreatic duct investigation by a technique called ERCP—endoscopic retrograde cholangiopancreatography.

Kevin had come to feel more like a surgeon as the number and variety of procedures were added. His office hours became less as his time spent in the endoscopy suite at the hospital increased. He had not chosen surgery during his medical school training due to its time constraints on personal life. And now he found himself in a place similar to the one he had rejected several years earlier.

Increasing work demands inevitably had led to broken family promises. Concert tickets had gone unused, parties had gone unattended, tennis matches were solo affairs ... and even a kindergarten graduation had to be watched on VCR tape.

Their only remaining sacred commitment was their annual trek to Disney World that the children enjoyed so much.

So broken promises were a fact of life to Jennifer and the family, as they are to most doctors' wives. And Jennifer excused it the best she could, considering what a wonderful provider and loving husband he had always been.

For Kevin, this busy lifestyle also had allowed flexibility in his personal schedule. He had quickly discovered that attractive women paid him more attention while behind the wheel of his sports car. And this had added new adventure to his life too personal to share even with his wife.

*   *   *   *

Evansville, N.C.—December 1, 2004

Mike Herman had never considered himself a ladies man and consequently had never had time for women in the past. Prior to meeting Danielle, he had spent most of his waking hours in pursuit of his work. He had been zealously studious in college and medical school ... in fact, he had graduated *magna cum laude* from college, where he had been elected to membership in *Phi Beta Kappa.* He had been in the top ten of his medical school class, earning him membership in *Alpha Omega Alpha* as well.

Prior to the one evening spent with Danielle Morgan, he had never been intimate with a woman. This sudden sexual encounter was a bit frightening to a previously confirmed bachelor.

While he enjoyed the physical part of the relationship, he found the companionship and closeness and feeling of being wanted ... and needed, almost as exhilarating.

He had tried to analyze his feelings since that evening, and he knew that he had to call Danielle back ... that he had to see her again soon. It was important to know that she felt the same way.

Still he remained a bit confused. He waited the whole day ... dialing ... hanging up, before he finally had her on the line. And then, hearing her voice, it was as if time had stood still since he last saw her face.

"Oh, Mike, it's *so* good to hear your voice. I've missed you so. I was afraid that things moved along a little too fast the other evening ... and that you might not want to see me again.

I want you to know that you don't have to feel pressured by what happened. If you want to see other people, I'll understand. I want you to know that this is kind of new for me too."

"I must confess that it unnerved me a bit ... I guess I'm not supposed to say that, being a man. But you know, I'm a little old fashioned. I still believe in taking things one step at a time.

But honestly, you're all I've thought about since the other night. I was hoping that if you're free this weekend, we might go away somewhere together ... maybe the coast?"

"Oh, that would be perfect. I'm not working and I can't think of anything I'd rather do than spend it with you.

You know, I know a cottage at the beach that we could rent. Availability shouldn't be a problem at this time of year."

"That would be great ... I don't know too much about the coastal area of North Carolina, so I'll leave the arrangements to you."

"You know, I **really** enjoyed the other night. I can't wait to see you again."

She knew exactly what to say ... exactly what Mike needed to hear.

"Neither can I. I'll call you tomorrow and you can give me all the details. Then we'll decide what time to leave on Friday."

*   *   *   *

"Hi, **Sis**. It took a few days, but he just called and asked me to spend the weekend with him. I told him that I knew a place at the beach and that I would make the arrangements.

So what would you like me to do?"

"Just leave everything to me, Danielle. Come over later and I'll tell you exactly what I'd like you to do. You know that you can always count on your big **sister** to take care of things."

Chapter 19

Evansville, N.C.—May 2004

Linda Young had just finished talking with her sister, who once again reminded her of obligations made long ago, when there was a knock on the back door.

Russ entered by the rear door dressed in old clothes. He drove his old car to minimize recognition, and parked a block or two away from her house, walking the remaining distance. He varied his parking places and walking route with each visit.

Linda ushered him into the kitchen where the atmosphere was instantly tense. She wanted to hear that he was ready to leave his wife, but she didn't dare raise her hopes too high.

Visions of ***High Noon*** danced in her head as she became aware of the ticking clock, a noise that enhanced the inhospitable feeling.

He gave her a light kiss on the cheek, remaining silent as he did. She returned the kiss in similar fashion and assumed the worst. There was no familiar close embrace.

"I'm afraid that we can't keep going on like this. It's not fair to you or me … or to the people we love.

You know that I care for you … deeply … but I'm not ready to make ***that*** commitment just yet."

Her heart sank in her chest. She tried to speak, but her throat was too parched for words to escape.

Hearing the words spoken imparts a finality somehow different than imagining them.

"We've meant so much to each other this past year. But I think the strain is starting to show on both of us, and I'm finding it hard to hide it from my family and my colleagues at work."

She immediately began weeping and hurled herself onto the couch. After all, what other emotion can erode a man's confidence or cause him to doubt his decision more than a woman's tears?

He sat down beside her and offered comfort by putting his arm around her shoulders. He found a box of tissues and sat quietly as she wiped her eyes.

She quickly regained her composure, and continued without apparent emotion.

"Of course, you are right. We have others to think of. But I'd prefer if we can remain friends."

A trite expression, perhaps, but *sister* had taught her to control her emotions and assess each situation … and make the best of it.

He expected her to remain more emotional. But he knew that the situation was still potentially explosive and that he had better not be flippant with his answer. He chose his words carefully.

"Of course.

I'd like that, too. We'll never stop feeling about each other what we've felt this past year. We can't throw that away."

She didn't respond. Instead, she just let his words stand, imagining how this scene might fit into future plans.

"Well, I'll see you at the hospital then" she said, as she stood up. He took that as his cue to leave.

"I won't forget our times together. And thanks for being so understanding", he added.

Things had gone well, he thought.

Perhaps too well.

* * * *

Linda went to the phone as soon as she heard the slam of the door. She called *sister* and reported the encounter in full detail.

Sister was furious.

How could Linda be so incompetent? Hadn't she taught her better? She told her that her inability to handle men *might* just have jeopardized the whole plan … and then she slammed the phone down onto the cradle.

But as she considered the situation, common sense prevailed. Perhaps this was even better. Perhaps they could use this aborted affair to their advantage ... at the appropriate time.

Sister called her back.

"My dear sweet Linda. I know that you did your best in a difficult situation ... and you're probably hurting right now. Forgive me for yelling at you the way I did. Please come to lunch and we can talk about it then ... just the two us. What do you say?"

She knew the invitation would appease her ... it always did.

"I'd really like that. I'll be over just as soon as I fix my face."

Linda dressed for a pleasant visit with her *sister*.

* * * *

A talk with *sister* always made her feel better, and especially this time. She was assured that things would probably work out even better than originally planned.

She had done her part well with Russ. She was attractive and alluring and accommodating to his every desire. And she had held the affair in strictest confidence, unlike many of her co-workers. She was frankly appalled at their willingness to divulge the most intimate secrets to anyone who would listen, including strangers.

Now she would have to await his next move ... that undoubtedly would soon come ... and *sister's* instructions.

She went to bed that evening excited about the intricate moves that she knew *sister* would plan. She was amazed at her ability to manipulate people's lives.

Sleep came easily with the knowledge that all would soon be well. After all, *sister* had told her so!

* * * *

Midsouth—June 2004

During the month following their breakup, there had been the usual work encounters and limited "hellos" but nothing more.

Suddenly, Russ stood in the doorway of the deserted employees' lounge in the x-ray department late one evening.

"Hi, gorgeous" he said, as he leaned over and gave her a kiss. He sat and took her hand.

"I've missed you so.

I don't know how I ever thought that I could get along without you?

I still can't promise when ... but I promise you that I will leave my family for you as soon as the time is right ... if you'll have me back?

I love you."

"Oh, Russ."

Tears streamed down her cheek. She checked her purse for a tissue.

He gave her his handkerchief.

"I thought you'd never come to your senses.

You know I'll wait for you ... forever if I must. But you must come over this weekend. We've got a lot of making up to do."

"You know I'll be there. It can't come soon enough."

He gave her a lingering kiss.

"I've got to get back to work ... so I'll see you Saturday." He disappeared around the corner.

"**Sister** is always right about men. They do know a good thing when they see it.

But, stupid creatures that men are, they don't always see what they think they see."

*   *   *   *

He took his usual clandestine approach to Linda's house.

Her preparations had been made in accordance with *sister's* instructions. And so, the couple would enjoy the day ... albeit for different reasons.

*   *   *   *

The knock came at the back door.

She admitted him quickly and feverishly the two embraced.

"I've missed you," she said.

"And I've missed you, too." They shared a deep kiss as she led him into the bedroom.

"I've prepared things *especially* for you."

CHAPTER 20

▼

Midsouth—October 2005

"He's seen a lot of my *project* charts, and he's asked me about the possibility of falsified pathology reports. I don't know exactly what he knows or suspects at this time ... but we need to put a stop to it or he could jeopardize the whole thing."

"Don't worry, my dear. Everything is under control. We've arranged a little surprise for him when he gets home from Boston. I think he'll get the message that he needs to back off. You know that I don't leave any loose ends when I plan something."

"All too well."

*   *   *   *

Evansville, N.C.—December 3, 2004

Mike and Danielle's big weekend had finally arrived. With the help of her *sister,* the arrangements had *all* been made.

Mike had borrowed a *Jeep* from one of his colleagues in pathology. It would be far mores suitable for the coastal sandy terrain than his old beat up station wagon ... not to mention sexier and sportier.

He picked her up early that Friday afternoon. It had been so long since he had been at the beach that he only vaguely remembered the smell of the ocean breeze or the sounds of waves crashing onto the shore.

The drive to the coast would take about four hours since most of the roads were two lanes and relatively old. Being off-season, at least it wouldn't be bumper to bumper like in the middle of the summer.

Danielle suggested they stop en route at a favorite spot, the **Beacon** restaurant, so-named because of the lighthouse shaped structure that sat atop the main restaurant.

"Why don't you order for the both of us while I go to the restroom", Mike suggested.

"It's been a long drive and I drank too much coffee at work today."

By the time he returned, the drinks were on the table. Moments later the food was served. And Danielle had been right ... it was good. In fact, the strawberry pie was some of the best he had had ... anywhere ... even at home.

"You certainly know how to pick a good place to eat, and I should know since my parents own a restaurant in Philadelphia.

You know, although I'm Greek, I've really come to love Southern cooking since moving to Evansville."

"Herman certainly doesn't sound Greek to me. But then ... there are a lot of things that I don't know about you. Hopefully, we can remedy that this weekend."

She took his arm and held his hand as he spoke.

"Actually, I was born in Athens, but my family moved to Philadelphia when I was three. My real name is Miklos Hermanopoulos; the family Americanized the name right after our arrival."

He summarized his family history for her.

"There!

Now you know everything about me. So tell me about you. Are you from Evansville, or do you come from some far off exotic place?"

Danielle recoiled from his questions momentarily. After a brief hesitation, she answered him.

"Heavens, no!

There's not much to tell actually. I was born in a small town near Raleigh, but my parents were both killed in an auto accident when I was little. So one of my aunts ... my father's sister ... raised me in the western part of the state. I had just finished training when I heard about job openings in radiology at Midsouth.

So there's just me ... no brothers or sisters, and my aunt died last year.

I was married once as I told you that day at the lake when we met. We never had children, so I live alone ... except for my cat, **Gizmo**. I really haven't dated much since my divorce."

Mike tightened his hold on her hand momentarily.

"You don't have to go into any detail about your personal life if you'd rather not. We can discuss that some other time if you like.

I like you for what I see now ... so there's plenty of time for your past later."

His gentleness and understanding impressed her immensely.

"You are most kind and unusually considerate.

I like that in a man."

Perhaps we should get back on the road. I'd like to be in time for you to see the sunset at the beach. It's usually quite spectacular."

Mike gleaned the sensuality in her voice and mannerism.

"Yes, I think it is time we got going." He paid the waitress and they got back into the *Jeep*.

*   *   *   *

Dusk was approaching as they arrived at the coast. Danielle directed him to the cottage, a two-story home built on stilts to protect it from tides and weather. It was located on a cul-de-sac across the street from the oceanfront ... **ocean-*view*** as the real estate people would describe it.

It was otherwise plain, but well kept by its owners.

Being late in the season, the neighboring homes were sparsely occupied. The rhythmic pounding of the surf in the distance was the only noise to be heard. The moon hung low over the horizon, casting eerie shadows along the row of beach houses, as it climbed to take its place among the stars. A light breeze intermittently blew into shore.

It turned out to be an unusually warm December day as so often happens along the southeast shore.

"What a beautiful setting. Let's just throw our things into the cottage and take a stroll along the beach" offered Mike.

"Perfect" replied Danielle.

"By the way, my friends call me Danni ... with an *I*," she intimated to him.

"I don't use it at work since people usually expect to see a man when they hear that name."

"Well then, Danni, let's take that stroll on the beach. I'm anxious to get my feet wet in the sand ... something I haven't done since I was a kid.

And I can't think of anyone I'd rather have at my side."

"The water will be cold, even though the day was fairly warm."

"That's o.k. As long as I'm with you … well, you know the old saying: warm heart … warm hands … warm feet."

He placed his arm around her shoulder as they made their way from the cottage. They removed their shoes as they approached the sand.

"The glow of dusk and the moon hanging over the horizon is even more beautiful than you would have led me to believe," he said.

It was a night made for lovers. The moon's light, now becoming more intense with the sun's demise, lit their way along the surf's edge. The warmth of the day quickly abated with the clear night sky and gentle breeze. As they walked, they stopped to experience the ebb and flow of the tide against their feet tentatively planted in the ever-shifting sands.

Mike took Danni into his arms and kissed her. His hand caressed the curvature of her head and held her ever closer and tighter to his hungry lips. She took his hand and placed it on her breast.

"Perhaps we should find a more private place," she whispered to him. Passion boiled in both their bodies, now surging with desire.

At the cottage, they immediately engaged in passionate lovemaking, even more intense than the night of the Davidson party.

And on their street, a light could now be seen in the house next door.

*   *   *   *

Evansville, N.C.—October 2004

For most of their friends, colleagues and co-workers at Midsouth, the wedding announcement that appeared in the Evansville Gazette that day in mid-October came as a total surprise. She had had her share of men, and one prior engagement; he was shy and reserved around women. It appeared to be a mismatch to most.

But there it was: Sarah Katherine Coleman and David Alton Fortner engaged to be married on Saturday, December 18, 2004.

It went on to say that the bride-to-be was formerly of Little Mountain, North Carolina and that her parents were deceased. The prospective groom was the son of the late Martin L. Fortner and Nicole Fortner Williams, now remarried, of Troy, New York.

The pending nuptials were fodder for gossip in and around the medical center. While Sarah was known to be extravagant, Dave was generally frugal.
He was at least ten years older than she.
Sarah drove a Mercedes convertible while Dave had a small older Buick.
Just what the secret attraction between them was, no one knew for sure. But it was fun to speculate.
And speculate they did.

*   *   *   *

"Well, I see that congratulations are in order.
Does this let me off the hook?"
"No. It's merely part of the plan to keep things in-house.
I'll let you know when you're off the hook … if ever.
We'll be seeing you at the wedding, I presume?"
"Of course. I wouldn't miss it for the world."
He reached under his desk for the bottle of Maalox and took a long pull from the neck.

*   *   *   *

Evansville, N.C.—December 18, 2004

Following a traditional wedding at the First Lutheran Church of Evansville, the reception was held at the York County Country Club. It was hailed as the social event of the Christmas season. Medical and nursing personnel, and members of the Midsouth administration staff had been invited to attend, in addition to immediate family members and assorted friends.

Neither the bride nor the groom had confided much concerning the details of the engagement or wedding plans to their co-workers. But somehow the fact that Sarah's gown was an original purchased in one of the fashion houses of New York had become public knowledge.

The major topic of the post-nuptial affair concerned the amount of work that would be necessary for Dave Fortner to pay for his wife's excesses.

*   *   *   *

Upon their return to Evansville from a honeymoon on board a chartered private yacht that had cruised the Caribbean, the couple moved from their respective apartments into a newly purchased older home in the fashionable country club section of town.

While the Fortners remained reclusive following the marriage, visitors to the country club area couldn't help but notice the changes taking place at their home. The stucco walls were redone in Williamsburg Gray with red trim shutters. A separate entertainment room was added to the rear of the home; the two structures were connected by an angled enclosed walkway that housed original paintings and art works. French doors in the entertainment room opened onto a patio with a figure eight swimming pool in the center. And a multilevel deck led from the poolside back into the gourmet kitchen in the main house.

The three acres of land surrounding the house were completely relandscaped. Wrought iron fencing was added to enclose the entire compound. Automatic gates marked the entrance and automated nocturnal illumination showcased it to the citizens of Evansville.

The compound was befitting of a cover page from **Better Homes and Gardens or Architectural Digest,** rivaling the most opulent homes in Evansville … and in much larger cities around the country for that matter.

*   *   *   *

Midsouth—February 2005

Mike was ill prepared for what was coming his way next.

He had enough things on his plate already, just taking care of things at the hospital. His latest lab project was all consuming … as had all the previous ones been. Except now he continued to make time for Danielle.

He didn't have time for unexpected or unwanted things in his life.

The weekend they had spent at the beach had been incredible … easily the most pleasurable of his life. They had shared each other's bodies … and minds … exchanging personal stories each had never allowed others to hear before. And while they spoke of doing things together in the near future, neither dared to suggest anything of a more permanent nature.

Mike still wasn't prepared for anything more binding; and Danielle had made it clear at their initial meeting that she was not interested in giving up the freedom that she had just earned with her divorce ... at least, not yet.

When she called him late one afternoon insisting on coming to his office, Mike assumed that she was just lonely, or wanted to bring him dinner as she frequently did. While their relationship was not a secret, he preferred that she only come after hours.

Her approach was a little hesitant.

She came in wearing her usual smile, gave him a kiss and took her seat.

"Mike, I hope this comes as good news for you as it has for me. I've been feeling a little queasy for the past few weeks.

Oh hell!

Mike, I'm pregnant!

There, I said it."

He sat in stunned silence. What does a man do when he suddenly feels trapped ... when he finds himself boxed in a canyon with the only way out guarded by the enemy?

He momentarily wished he were a little boy again ... that he could run to his mother or father for protection. But that was not possible. He was a big boy now, and big boys are responsible for their own actions.

The silence continued for what seemed an eternity for both.

How could I let this happen? Wasn't she taking the pill? Why didn't I ask her? I trusted her, that's why.

What next? Marriage ... a baby ... or, God forbid ... an abortion? Not my child!

She's here for my opinion and advice ... that's it.

After only a few seconds that seemed like an eternity, he began to speak.

"I'm not sure what to say ... I mean, I guess all along I thought you were taking precautions not to get pregnant. We never really discussed that.

And how do you feel about being pregnant?"

"I'm not sure how I feel, Mike. But I knew I had to discuss it with you before making any further decisions."

"I assume you've done a pregnancy test. There's no possibility that it could be falsely positive, is there?"

"I did it twice ... I had to convince myself as well."

"Danni, don't take this the wrong way ... but there's no possibility that it could be someone else's, is there?"

He knew the minute the words left his lips that the question was insensitive and thoughtless. He hated himself for having thought it, let alone having said it out loud.

He came to her and put his arm around her as she began to cry.

"Oh Mike, you know that there hasn't been anyone but you …"

He interrupted her.

"Danni, I love you and I want us to have this baby. If you'll have me, I think that we should slip over the border to South Carolina and get married right away. After all, a baby needs a father too!"

"Oh Mike."

Her face was radiant again. She looked him squarely in the face and gave him a deep passionate kiss.

"I was so hoping that's what you would say. I want the baby too.

Are you sure about getting married?"

"I knew that I was in love with you the day we met at the lake. And I knew since the weekend we spent at the beach that I wanted to marry you. But you know, we shy bachelors have a way of taking our time with some things."

"Then can we go back to the house and discuss it some more? I'll fix us dinner."

"Sounds great. But let me finish this one last slide in the set I was working on. Then we can go and celebrate the good news." He gave her a kiss.

"I'm going to wait by your secretary's desk while you finish."

She whispered, "I love you" as she walked to the door.

He smiled.

"How quickly life changes" he thought. He felt good about his decision.

*　　*　　*　　*

"It went even better than we planned. He took it all very well and reacted as you predicted he would. You now, he's really a nice guy. Wedding bells will be ringing soon."

"And we need this nice guy for our plans."

"We won't need to use the backup plan just yet … I'll try to talk him into joining us."

"Good work, Danielle", said **sister**.

*　　*　　*　　*

At home that evening over dinner, they decided on taking a long weekend trip to the beach and slipping over the state line to South Carolina to get married. Fortunately, their neighboring state believed in quick weddings. That way, they could hopefully avoid the inevitably embarrassing questions about the timing of the baby's birth relative to the wedding.

Besides, they were in love ... or so Mike thought.

Chapter 21

▼

Evansville, N.C.—October 17, 2005

They caught the first available flight back to Evansville early the following morning. The ride from the airport was unmercifully long given the circumstances that brought them home early.

They drove directly to Jack's office where they found only the smoldering, charred remains of what had been "home" for fifteen years. It was far worse seeing it in person than either could have imagined from the information given them on the phone.

They had hoped that something might be salvaged ... but from what they could see, it was a total loss.

The fire had apparently started during the night. The alarm had not functioned; so it was early morning before someone noticed smoke coming from the building. By the time the fire department arrived, it had burst into flames and was beyond salvage. All they could do was prevent it from spreading to surrounding structures that stood nearby.

Several members of the fire crew were still present as Jack and Lynn approached. They were combing the debris for clues and making sure that no embers remained active enough to cause a new eruption of flames.

Jack approached the apparent officer in charge.

"Hi. I'm Dr. Davidson. This is ... **was** ... my office." His voice crackled as he spoke the words.

"Any idea what happened?"

"It's good to meet you, although I'm sorry it has to be under these circumstances.

I'm Sergeant Miller from the Evansville Fire Department arson squad. We're here collecting evidence along with the police department. We're not quite finished, so I can't give you any definite answers.

I've been asked to have you call Captain Leonard at the Evansville Police Department. His section handles potential arson cases. I'm sure he has some questions he wants to ask you."

"Do you mean to imply that this fire was deliberately set?" Jack asked incredulously.

"I'm not at liberty to say at this point, since the investigation isn't complete. The police and our people are assimilating information. But I do know that the fire alarm was disabled.

Let me give you Captain Leonard's number so that you can contact him as soon as possible. And you should contact your insurance carrier as soon as you can. They will undoubtedly want to send their own inspectors."

Jack was reeling.

"Arson? Disabled alarm?"

Who could possibly want to do something like this? And why?

Or could it possibly have been meant for someone else? Maybe they targeted the wrong building and it was all a mistake.

Perhaps they were looking for drugs and when they didn't find any, they decided to torch the place.

The thoughts raced through Jack's head.

He had heard of stories like that.

He thanked Sergeant Miller.

The couple got back into the car.

"Lynn, let's go talk to this Captain Leonard right now. I want to know what he knows."

He called the captain on his cell phone and arranged to meet immediately.

*　　*　　*　　*

"Please come in and have a seat."

After seating the couple, he introduced himself.

"I'm Captain Gerald Leonard.

Dr. Davidson, although we've never met, I'm quite aware of your reputation as one of Evansville's finest surgeons. So while it's a pleasure to meet you and Mrs. Davidson, I'm especially sorry that it has to be under such circumstances.

Losing a home or business is bad enough … but to have it happen while out of town must be particularly distressing."

"Yes", replied Jack.

"Do you have any idea how the fire started?"

"Of course we're waiting for all the pieces of evidence from the scene to be collected and analyzed. I think that Sergeant Miller already apprised you of the progress in the investigation.

And I think he indicated … and I think it is fair of me to say too … that it appears to have been deliberately set …"

Before he could even finish the sentence, Jack interrupted him.

"You mean it was definitely arson? Who in the world would want to do something like that to me?

Do you have any evidence to suggest who might be involved?"

"Please, Dr. Davidson. I know that this must come as a shock to you and your wife, as it should to anyone. It's very disconcerting to think that someone may be out there who wants to do you harm or make you suffer.

But I need to ask you some questions … in fact, the very questions that you just asked me.

Do you know of anyone who might want to harm you … or possibly someone in your office?

We can't yet determine if robbery could have been a motive since there is little left intact. We'll need a list of things you had in your office that could have been a target for a thief … perhaps something that he could fence … that is exchange for money.

There's actually nothing to suggest anyone trying to inflict harm on you or your employees since it was done at night when the building was empty.

Could this have been some type of warning by someone carrying a grudge? I mean they …"

"What do you mean *they*?"

"Just a figure of speech, Doc. We don't know if it is *he* or *she* or *they* at this point."

Jack tried to calm himself down before proceeding.

"Of course. How silly of me. I can't think of anyone who would resort to something like this.

Most members of my profession probably have a disgruntled patient or family member from time to time, although I'm not aware of any now or in recent months.

But burn my office down!

No, I can't think of anyone who would fit that category."

"And how about you, Mrs. Davidson? Do you recall anyone who might carry a grudge against your husband?"

She thought for a few moments.

"I'm not personally involved in running the office, although I try to keep up with what's going on. The girls at the office haven't said anything to me about any untoward comments or threats. I'm not aware of anyone getting annoyed about their bills ... though that can get people quite irritated from time to time."

"And how about your employees? Are you aware of any interpersonal problems at home? Sometimes, a pending separation or divorce will get people really mad, causing them to do things they ordinarily wouldn't do."

The couple both answered with negative head motions.

"On the other hand, they did disarm the alarm system. So we probably have to assume it was aimed at you or something in your office.

We'll be checking every detail, you can be sure. So you can help by providing us a list of all your employees and an inventory of the things that were in your office ... at least, as best you can.

Be sure to include peripheral contacts such as janitorial services, lab pickup people ... any regular visitor to your office who may not be an employee, but who would know your setup and your office routine.

Now, in the meantime, I would recommend that you two go home and get some rest and collect your thoughts. I'm sure that it has been a long and distressing day. Give me a call later when you get things together.

And if you think of anything you deem important, call me anytime. Otherwise, we'll be in touch soon." He handed Jack one of his personal business cards. He had written his home and cell phone numbers on the back.

They thanked him for his help and personal interest, and assured him that they would call if anything new or different occurred to them.

The ride home was somber. They were both numbed by the day's events, and fatigued since starting the day extremely early in New England and winding up home looking at the office remains.

And the thought of **why** and **who** kept running through both their heads.

"People always say that after your home is robbed, you feel violated and helpless. I feel the same way right now, not knowing why this is happening to us.

How about you?"

"I'm a little frightened, too, Honey", he answered.

"I guess it's the fact that we don't have any answers yet that makes it all so upsetting

And I keep thinking about this investigation that I'm working on for the hospital. I wonder about a possible connection. But from what I've uncovered so far, there would have to be far more to it. I'd have to be chasing something awful big to warrant this."

"Why didn't you mention it to Captain Leonard?"

"At this point I don't really have much ... some reports suggesting possible collusion, but no real hard facts. And certainly nothing that would warrant someone burning down my office.

If I can get something more concrete, I'll let Captain Leonard in on it."

"I'd feel much better about it if you did. If this was meant to scare us ... it's sure worked on me. And I'm concerned about your safety.

Now, let's get home and have something to eat and get some rest. It'll still be there in the morning when ... hopefully ... our heads will be clearer."

As they turned into the driveway, Jack activated the automatic garage door opener, and proceeded into the garage.

Much to their horror, suspended from the light fixture, was their eight year old cocker spaniel, **Bonkers**, dead. Someone had placed a rope around the poor animal's neck.

*   *   *   *

"Jack, Bill Smithson is on the phone. He'd like to talk to you", said Lynn.

"Hi, Bill."

"Jack, I just heard about your office fire and I'd like to see if there is some way I can help. The hospital has some space available in one of our buildings near the hospital that you are welcome to use temporarily if it meets your needs.

Have the police or fire department been able to determine anything yet about the cause of the fire ... although, I guess it's probably too soon?" he said, answering his own question.

Jack confirmed his assumption. He felt it best in the light of the day's activities and surprises not to divulge any information, especially in regard to possible arson.

"The authorities are still working at the site. They are supposed to let us know something as soon as they can about the cause. In the meantime, we are just trying to pick up the pieces the best we can.

We just got back from Boston a few hours ago. How about letting me look at it with you in the morning? I'm going to be meeting with my office staff later in the morning, so if it's workable, they'll want to come by to see the building afterward.

Fortunately, my office manager is a fanatic about keeping backup computer discs away from the office. So she has copies of all our patient records and billing information at her home. I used to think that was a waste of time ... that something like this could never happen to me. I'm certainly glad that she has proven me wrong. This whole thing is like a nightmare being played out in slow motion.

And Bill, thanks again for your concern and your most generous offer."

"Well, if there's anything I can do for you or Lynn, please feel free to call on me or Maggie or my staff. I think we can probably arrange some furnishings for the office as well if you like.

I'll look forward to seeing you in the morning."

*　　*　　*　　*

Jack and Lynn faced each other. She had a frightened look on her face as tears began to roll down her cheek.

"Jack, I'm scared.
First the office, and now poor **Bonkers** too.
Who could be doing this to us?
Who in the world would want to harm us, and why?"

"I don't know, Honey. I feel like we're characters in the middle of a horror movie script, except that I know that it won't be ending in an hour or two.
In fact, the ending may not have been written yet!
And now this is definitely personal. Few people would know to harm a pet."

He sat next to her and put his arm around her shoulders and drew her into himself. He gave her a kiss as he attempted to console her.

"Something big must be going on at the hospital that I've accidentally stumbled into. Someone is sure going to great lengths to scare us away ... if indeed that's what's going on.

I think we had better be careful who we talk to and what we say from now on."

"Don't you think you should tell Captain Leonard about **Bonkers?**" Lynn asked, tears still streaming.

"Not just yet.
Let's wait until it's confirmed about the arson. If the fire was an accident, then this may be just a silly coincidence ... a bad joke played by a kid or someone mad at us for some reason.

Now, why don't you make us some coffee while I bury **Bonkers?** Then I think we should get some rest ... we both have had a long day."

"Are you sure you should bury her without the police seeing her remains first? That poor innocent creature. Humans can be so cruel."

"I'll bury her in the back yard. They can always retrieve her later if necessary."

While he performed the odious task, he vowed to avenge the misdeed.

"Let cooler heads prevail. We'll find out who did this ... then we'll show them who's smarter."

He returned to the house and the waiting coffee.

* * * *

The next morning Jack was about his usual business at the hospital before eight o'clock. He was a little later than usual since he wasn't originally scheduled to be in town. But he had left a few patients behind and was there to check on their status.

By now the story of the office fire had made the local papers and had spread around the medical complex.

"Jack, sorry to hear about the office. Anything I can do to help?" was a line he heard dozens of times that day.

He made his way to the I.C.U. where Elaine and Sharon were waiting for him. These two favorites of his rushed over to express their concern for the situation ... and to jokingly offer to quit their jobs and come help him ... something they did not infrequently.

"You know that I'd give my surgeon's right arm to have the two of you working for me. But I can't afford to pay you what you're worth. Besides, we need you both right here."

They smiled.

"And besides, you two would get bored with the humdrum of an office after working here all these years."

Elaine notified him of a consult. He reviewed the patient's chart and then asked her to accompany him while he interviewed and examined the elderly lady.

She had been admitted the night before for a presumed heart attack. But all the tests for cardiac disease had been normal. She now complained of abdominal pain and nausea. Jack concluded after his examination that she most likely was having a gallbladder attack.

"Since she's been vomiting, I think we'd better use an NG tube on her."

"I've already got an 18 Salem Sump at the bedside. Constant suction, right?"

"You know my routine almost as well as me.
Perfect," he replied.
"And we'll need a gallbladder ultrasound."
"I already checked with x-ray and they can do it in about thirty minutes."
"You should have been a doctor", he said to his worthy nursing colleague.
He finished the orders and then went to dictate his consult note.
"Well ladies. I'm off to the office ... or rather to meet my staff and see what's left of it, and to make some arrangements for a temporary location.
But first I have a meeting with Dr. Smithson to look at some space the hospital has available."

* * * *

Martha, Bill's secretary, was awaiting his arrival. She expressed her concern about his situation and then ushered him right into Bill's office.
"Dr. Smithson, Dr. Davidson is here."
"Come in, Jack.
Have you heard any more news this morning?"
"Not from the police or fire department. I did talk to my insurance agent and he assured me that we should be able to begin rebuilding within thirty to sixty days. They're going to send an inspector out today to survey things."
Jack sat for a few minutes unloading some of his burdens on Bill, but being careful not to divulge any of the speculation about arson.
"It's a terrible thing that happened, but let's see if we can help you get back in business."
Bill buzzed Martha from his office.
"I'm going to walk Dr. Davidson over to the rental property on Metropolitan Drive. I should be back within the hour."
Metropolitan Drive lay towards the rear of the medical campus. Midsouth had been acquiring properties adjacent to the original hospital for years. As the campus had expanded, many neighborhood homes had been purchased and converted into rental office space for physicians as well as peripheral hospital services such as home health and hospice.
The property that Bill had in mind for Jack's temporary office was one such converted home that had been used by a staff neurologist who had just moved into his own newly constructed facility.
"Jack, this will give you about eighteen hundred square feet of usable space" he said as they entered the waiting room portion.

"It's not what you're used to, I'm sure. But it's clean and near the hospital." They finished inspecting all the rooms and then returned to the entrance.

"It will be a bit small compared to my old office. But considering our situation, I'm sure it can work. It will be nice and handy, being so close to the hospital.

I'm meeting with my staff as soon as we're through here. Perhaps I can bring them by afterward and see what they think. We can let you know something by this afternoon."

"It certainly can't compare with your old office" ... he knew what a showplace Jack's old office was ... "but you're welcome to use it until you can rebuild your own office."

"I'll call you later", Jack said as he departed for the meeting with his staff.

* * * *

They came by and inspected it with him at the conclusion of their brief meeting. All agreed that it would be small but workable ... and it was immediately available. So they could get going right away trying to reestablish business.

"Bill, we'll take it." Jack called him on his cell phone from the rental property.

"Great", said Bill.

"We'll work out the business details later. And let me know if there is anything else you need in the way of furniture or supplies."

* * * *

Bill accessed his private line and dialed the number.
"It's all set. You know what to do."

* * * *

Jack was methodically working on meeting with various office staff members and his accountant to assess the business's future needs and to plan for a new office building that undoubtedly would have to be smaller.

Jack left the staff working on the office details while he drove by the remains of his former office, wondering again why someone ... anyone ... would want to do this to him and his family ... **him** of all people. To his knowledge, he hadn't harmed anyone. He was competitive in business, but fair. He didn't know of any enemies among his colleagues.

And who would want to kill a perfectly innocent animal like **Bonkers?** It obviously had to be someone he knew ... someone who knew about his dog.

Jack kept running the whole thing through his mind: patients, colleagues, business dealings ... and always he came back to the same name: ***Dave Fortner***.

It was the only name that made any sense.

"If I'm on to something, who knows what I already know? It has to be one of the people I've already talked to: Russ Callahan or Mike Herman ... or one of the people in their department handling the reports.

But what's their part in it and how are they connected to Dave Fortner?"

Answering a question with a question. It was becoming more confusing and more frightening ... not knowing who could be trusted.

Finally, he decided he would call one of the people he was sure he could trust: Frank Li.

"We're good friends. Besides, he has his finger on the pulse of the hospital in the Emergency Department. Frank always knows what's going on around here."

He called Frank and arranged to meet him later that afternoon.

"*If* Dave Fortner is behind this, I swear I'll get the son-of-a-bitch!"

Chapter 22

Evansville, N.C.—October 2005

"Lord, how long does it take?
 I need to know.
 Me ... Katie Moore!
 Here I am, all alone except for my two sisters, Janie and Marie ... and our hellish memories.
 Finally, it's our turn to do what we knew one day we would have to do.
 Why did our parents treat us that way?
 Why were we different from other little girls our age?
 Didn't they love us ... even a little?
 Why couldn't the others in town see the way they abused us?
 I hate these professional people ... these ***doctors***. They're just like daddy was ... they don't care!
 Well, since Daddy is no longer with us, it's their turn to suffer. And suffer they will for the sins of our father!"

Chapter 23

▼

Dr. Susan Aldrich
Physician Complaint Division
North Carolina State Medical Board
Raleigh, N.C.

Dear Dr. Aldrich:

I am not sure if this letter is appropriate, but I am concerned about some issues regarding the medical care rendered me recently here in Evansville.

I was originally seen by my family doctor, Carl Hauser, for abdominal pain. The test he ordered to check for gallstones came back negative, and I was no longer having any abdominal pain. To my surprise, a few days later his office called and said they had made an appointment with a specialist and he would check out my problem. I told them I was feeling fine, but they insisted that I check with the specialist.

While seeing the specialist, Dr. Kevin Bledsoe, he told me that my gallbladder tests were positive for gallstones and he wanted me to have a special test done, an ERCP. That test made me very sick.

Based on that test, he told me I needed to see a surgeon and he referred me to Dr. Dave Fortner, who would remove my gallbladder. Because I got so sick after the ERCP, I decided that maybe I did have gallbladder problems and needed the surgery.

I am concerned because after talking with my cousin and several other acquaintances, I find that they had the same experience. They also were told that the first test was negative for gallstones by their family physician, but were referred to Dr. Bledsoe for the same test that I had, an ERCP. They all got sick with that test just like I did. Dr. Bledsoe referred all of them to Dr. Fortner to have their gallbladder removed just like me.

We are all wondering if we needed the surgery in the first place since we all felt good after the original gallbladder test that we were told was normal. We only felt bad after the ERCP.

It's scary that we all saw precisely the same group of doctors, and had the same tests and the same surgery.

Please let me know what you think.

Sincerely,

Carol Smith
201 Foxcroft Lane
Evansville, N.C.
October 13, 2005

P.S. I have the names of some other patients who had similar experiences with the same physicians. I can provide them to you if that would be of help.

"Caroline."

"Yes, Dr. Aldrich."

"I was just reading the letter from Mrs. Carol Smith that you left on my desk. Didn't we just have another very similar sounding letter mentioning the same names in Evansville?"

Caroline appeared in the door to her office.

"Yes. It was from a Mrs. Tina Rouse. She lives very near to Evansville and listed the same doctors and a very similar story."

"What do you think?"

"I'll see who the chief of surgery is down there and get him on the phone for you."

"Thank you."

*　　*　　*　　*

The events appeared purely random at first glance. Two different patients had filed letters with the physician complaint division of the N.C. State Medical Board, alleging possible mistreatment at the hands of the same group of doctors for virtually identical problems.

But it had not been entirely by accident.

Carol Smith and her cousin, Tina Rouse, had each sought help from their family physician, Dr. Carl Hauser, approximately one month apart. Neither was aware of the others' condition or visit to Dr. Hauser's office.

Each had seen him about vague abdominal pain of short duration. Each had been subjected to a gallbladder ultrasound. The results had been negative and each had been placed on medication.

Although their symptoms had disappeared, after only a few days each had been contacted and referred for gastroenterological consultation. Following an ERCP exam by Dr. Kevin Bledsoe, they were referred to Dr. Dave Fortner for gallbladder surgery.

The two encountered one another while shopping at the Evansville Mall. Though related, and living only twenty miles apart, they rarely saw each other more than once or twice a year.

While sharing a cup of coffee, Carol casually mentioned that she had had her gallbladder removed several months earlier by a Dr. Dave Fortner.

Further discussion led to the fact that both had seen the same three doctors, had the same evaluation including the ERCP, and then the gallbladder surgery by Dr. Fortner.

Carol commented that she found it strange that the ultrasound exam that was done initially was negative for gallstones. Yet, she had been referred to Dr. Bledsoe for an ERCP, usually done for stones in the bile duct ... she and her husband had done research about it on the Internet afterward.

"You know, Tina, the strange thing is that before the time I had that test done, I was feeling pretty good. After the test, I was sicker than a dog and couldn't wait to have the surgery."

Tina's experience had been almost identical.

"Dr. Bledsoe said the gallbladder test showed stones and indicated a bile duct problem, even though Dr. Hauser said mine was normal too.

My husband was not very satisfied with the way the whole thing was handled, although at the end I felt good. But I sure was sick for a while after that ERCP test."

They decided that perhaps they should discuss the matter further with their husbands present. They arranged to meet the following evening.

The husbands were both infuriated by the inconsistency of the reports concerning the presence or absence of gallstones, and the lack of clear indications for the ERCP that appeared to make both of the women ill. It prompted them to meet and discuss the situation with an attorney friend of Carol's, Matthew Gates.

He listened attentively to their stories, and then quickly and appropriately advised them that if they had not suffered any untoward consequences from the procedures that there would be little grounds for considering legal action.

They had had all the procedures discussed in detail and had signed consent forms. The disparity between the reported results of the various tests was unfortunate, but could have been simply poor communication between hospital and office or between the doctors themselves.

They could simply file a complaint with the hospital and/or the State Medical Board. There was a form available for the latter which he offered to obtain for them.

"We've already done that. So far we haven't had any response."

"I'm sure you'll hear something soon. The Medical Board is very conscientious about responding in a timely fashion. But they will undoubtedly request information from the doctors involved before responding to you. So you'll have to give them a little time."

He also advised them that if they preferred to pursue the matter further, they could obtain copies of their records from the doctors' offices and the hospital. He would be glad to review the records and advise them further.

They both liked this latter idea and obtained their records and delivered them to Matthew Gates' office for his review.

*   *   *   *

Two weeks after they had submitted the records to Matthew Gates' office, Carol and Tina were notified that he would like to meet with them to discuss his conclusions and recommendations.

Neither was sure if their concerns would be substantiated, but at least they would have an opinion by a neutral party.

Matthew had, on review of the records, substantiated the disparity between the results of their gallbladder tests as reported by the various doctors.

"How were each of you feeling between the time you saw Dr. Hauser and Dr. Bledsoe?"

Both replied that they were fine until having the ERCP done.

"Did either of you know or request Dr. Bledsoe or Dr. Fortner?"

Neither had.

Matthew hesitated, choosing the next words that he would utter very carefully.

"You both know that I don't usually handle matters that deal with medical problems.

Your stories are both so identical. The most disturbing part to me is the disparity of the test results and the fact that you both were ill after this ERCP test. That suggests to me that something untoward may have occurred as a result of that procedure that ultimately altered the outcome.

But keep in mind that we are only talking about two cases here ... a very small number to try to make any meaningful judgment. Perhaps if you knew some other people who had been operated on by this Dr. Fortner we could find others with a similar experience. Then we might have grounds on which to proceed with filing complaints."

"I've got a list of about six right here," Tina said, reaching into her purse."

"That'll be a start.

I might also suggest that a friend of mine from law school is an expert in such matters. He works for a large law firm in Raleigh that specializes in only medically related cases. If we can gather additional information, then you might want to get him involved.

Personally, I think you probably don't have much of a case, but I'd like to give you every opportunity to explore this. If there were some substance to it, I'm sure there are lots of people who would be interested to hear about it."

"So, what's our next move?" blurted out Tina.

"See if you can get some more cases in addition to the ones you just gave me. In the meantime, I'll contact my friend in Raleigh and run this by him. If he thinks it's worthy of pursuing, he'll tell me and I'll call you both.

By the way, his name is Bill Smithson, Jr. His father is CEO of Midsouth where you had your surgery. He hasn't lived in town for a number of years, so I'd consider him unbiased, and he'll know who to contact for additional information if necessary."

*   *   *   *

Matthew Gates called Bill Smithson, Jr. the morning following his meeting with Carol and Tina. He was a bit reluctant to get involved with matters that concerned Midsouth. But he agreed to help Matthew in this case and at least offer an opinion. Judging from the information presented to him by Matthew, he frankly doubted that it would go any farther than that.

*   *   *   *

As part of her follow up on the Smith and Rouse letters, Dr. Susan Aldrich had notified both of the women of her ongoing investigation and promised a follow-up letter as soon as a judgment had been rendered.

Her jurisdiction also included investigation of unexpected or unexplained in-hospital deaths. So, it was all the more disturbing when she heard of the death of a patient undergoing an ERCP at Midsouth ... with some of the same physicians again involved.

Her staff had quickly gone to work following protocol and requested additional information on the complaint cases. She was awaiting the final autopsy report before deciding the necessity for further action in the case of the ERCP death.

Her protocol demanded that the CEO of the institution be notified of the record request; so a copy was forwarded to Dr. Bill Smithson. He noted it with alarm.

It did little to help his ever-worsening stomach problem.

CHAPTER 24

Altamont, N.C.—1992

After their father's untimely death, the Moore sisters were forced to spend the remainder of their school days in the company of their stepmother. But as soon as the twins turned eighteen, the three had disappeared from home and begun life anew on their own. The nightmare that had been their former existence had suddenly ceased to exist. But the memories lingered, especially with Katie, the eldest. She had promised to avenge their father's actions and the stepmother's inattention and failure to intercede.

Katie had attended college in Boonesboro, in the western part of the state, and the twins had followed her there. Eventually, they chose to move together to a location that would afford them the opportunity to carry out the vicarious revenge against their father's profession.

Katie needed to release the hostility so long bottled up inside; Janie and Marie promised to be there when needed. They had taken the special photography courses at the insistence of Katie ... courses that would later prove invaluable.

* * * *

Midsouth—November 15, 2005

In spite of his distaste for this special task, Mike knew that he had to complete the autopsy on Alice Roddenberry, the patient who had died while undergoing the ERCP by Kevin Bledsoe. The gross findings had been relatively non-specific, so he would have to rely on the histologic and toxicologic results to formulate his conclusions.

Mike had organized and reviewed the slides prepared from the gross material; the blood samples taken immediately after death; and the special lab studies including toxicology reports and those done to screen for allergic reactions. **SEM** ... scanning electron microscopy ... had been performed on selected samples as well.

Tissue samples from the edematous larynx revealed that the mast cells in virtually every instance had undergone degranulation, indicative of massive histamine release. The cause was obscure since no allergies were listed. Peripheral blood smears and IgE levels were all essentially normal.

Routine slides prepared from the brain and kidney were normal. The lungs showed mild pulmonary edema consistent with post-intubation changes.

The abdominal contents presented more of a challenge for Mike. Since there was no overt evidence of any gallbladder or biliary tract disease, his diener would see to the necessary sample alterations. Mike would word his report to reflect those changes.

The toxicology report showed a detectable level of midazolam, the drug used to sedate the patient during the procedure. Several other drug trace amounts detected were undergoing additional tests to determine their significance, if any.

Mike needed these results and additional patient information in order to complete the report so that a final summary could be submitted to local authorities and the state medical board that required a copy for their records and review. The whole business was unnerving to him. He felt that he had already paid adequately for his indiscretion.

He had previously dispatched a clinical nurse specialist to seek additional information from surviving family members and reviewed her findings as well.

* * * *

MaryAnn Stephens, the clinical nurse specialist from Midsouth dispatched by Mike Herman, was sent to re-interview the family of the deceased. Patients and families under the stress of pending surgery or the death of a loved one often forget pertinent medical facts. The several week hiatus might be helpful in obtaining additional information.

MaryAnn knew how to look for facts about alcohol and drug abuse in the deceased, or the use of excess non-prescription drugs or borrowed prescription drugs.

Alice Roddenberry was forty-three years old at the time of her death. She left a husband and two children, ages eight and fourteen.

MaryAnn was thoroughly trained to handle delicate situations like this. She approached families slowly and sympathetically, letting them do the talking initially, allowing them to dissipate any hostility they might harbor against the hospital or doctors. Then she would direct her questions toward the matters that needed clarification.

At the Roddenberry home, things went much as she had anticipated. The husband expressed anger at the loss of his wife. He dwelled a while on his inability to raise the children by himself, and the burden it placed on him since he needed to work to support them. The family had no reserve savings and his wife's insurance money would barely pay for her funeral expenses.

He made no overture towards legal action against anyone.

When she sensed that the time was right, she proceeded with her questions.

"Mr. Roddenberry, I have been asked by Dr. Michael Herman, the pathologist who examined your wife's body, to review some elements of her medical history with you. According to the information that she provided to her doctor and to the nursing personnel before the procedure, she had no history of drug allergies and had not been taking any routine medications.

However, we have reason to believe that she may have taken some medications just prior to coming to the hospital for the ERCP test. Do you know if she kept any drugs here in the house?"

"My wife didn't use drugs ... she was a good wife to me and a good mother to our children."

"I'm sure she was, Mr. Roddenberry. I didn't mean to imply anything illegal. Sometimes people take prescription drugs and forget about them. And sometimes they take large amounts of non-prescription drugs that they don't think are important.

People often take medications because they are in chronic pain or they are afraid.

Was your wife in pain?"

"She had been complaining about her stomach for a long time. She had been to several doctors, but they couldn't find the problem. She was real nervous about having the test done the day she died. I think she might have taken some of the medication that I use for my back ... I have a disc problem. I can get them for you if you like."

"Yes. That would be very helpful, Mr. Roddenberry."

He disappeared into the hall bathroom and emerged with a handful of medication vials, all bearing his name.

MaryAnn made a list of the drugs: Darvocet-N, an analgesic or pain medication; diazepam, a muscle relaxant/tranquilizer. In addition, there were multiple vitamin supplements and the final one she looked at: Captopril, an anti-hypertensive or blood pressure medicine.

"Do you know if your wife was using any of these?" she asked.

"She was hurting real bad and was nervous right before we left for the hospital that morning, and took one of each. Then I checked her blood pressure with the cuff I use to monitor my own pressure and it was high … real high … so I told her to take one of these too", he added, pointing to the Captopril.

"She was afraid they wouldn't do the tests if her blood pressure was too high. She asked me not to say anything.

I hope that wasn't the wrong thing to do."

"Hopefully not, Mr. Roddenberry."

MaryAnn knew that the information was probably very important. But for the moment, she just played nurse and helped to soothe a heartbroken and lonely husband.

*   *   *   *

Evansville, N.C.—Summer 2005

Work is an elixir to some: both vocation and avocation.

For most members of the human race, it is a lifelong drudgery necessary to survive.

Sarah Coleman Fortner's family had had money, but rarely used it for anything pleasurable. She intended for her marriage to Dave Fortner to change all that … she had seen to it personally.

Dave's volume of business had increased substantially since their marriage thanks to her interventions. Sarah had continued her job part-time at Midsouth and devoted her off time to planning their every move, allowing Dave little say in business matters. His job, which he now clearly understood, was to keep the money flowing to support his wife's expensive habits.

She had submitted her resignation effective August 31, 2005 so that she could devote her full time to her various pursuits.

Remodeling their home had become her obsession. The kitchen had been redone with all the latest expensive appliances ... although she rarely cooked. Every light fixture had been replaced with new and expensive ones. Though no one played the piano, an eight-foot grand had been installed in the music room.

The exterior was no less imposing with lights illuminating the entire perimeter of their compound, now encircled with wrought-iron fencing. While Dave was forced to increase his workload commensurate with her spending, his personal tastes remained simple. He drove an old car and dressed conservatively. His one major passion and expense was his airplane. It allowed him an escape from the rigors of the hospital ... and home and Sarah. It afforded him a place to think and to relax for short periods of time.

And when he was alone, his thoughts frequently went back to that night in *Hana* ... and what it had come to represent. How often he wished that he had never heard the name ... *Hana* ... or even considered asking Sarah to go to the meeting in Hawaii that had started all this. The deal that had been struck there, had been reinforced in Evansville after their return.

Marriage is a contract based on trust ... not threats.

* * * *

Evansville, N.C.—November 20, 2005

Sarah reached over to answer the wall phone in the kitchen. She was savoring her coffee after her husband's departure for the hospital. She purposefully let it ring four times before picking it up ... it made her feel important to make people wait.

"Hi, sis, are you alone?"

"Yes", answered Sarah.

"There may be a problem brewing that I thought you would want to know about right away. Mike was working late last night when he ran into Jack Davidson. He followed him to medical records where Jack spent about three hours working on medical charts.

Mike looked at the charts that he had worked on ... and most of them are *project* patients. Of course, he is Chief of Surgery and could be working on something else. But considering the fact that he is working on a project about gallstones with the help of radiology, and that he asked Mike about faking reports in pathology, I think it's only logical to be concerned".

"Damn", said Sarah.

"I had hoped that our previous warnings would have scared him off by now. But I always suspected that he was too much of a do-gooder to give up very easily. I'll let the others know what's going on. In the meantime, just sit tight until we know something.

Good work!"

"Thanks, Sis."

                *   *   *   *

Dave had not yet reached the hospital when his cell phone rang.

"Jack Davidson has been looking at some of your records. Mike followed him to medical records last night and confirms that most of the charts were **project** patients, so I think we have to assume that he's absolutely on to us.

I guess we're going to have to do something else to discourage him, or everything we've worked for will come crashing down on us."

                *   *   *   *

His special line rang.

With each ring, knots formed in his stomach. He reached for the phone ... and his Rolaids simultaneously.

"Things are beginning to get a little hairy. It appears that he's on to us ... he's been sneaking around medical records reviewing charts of **project** patients.

We need to do something else before this goes any farther. He certainly doesn't scare easily ... I mean after the office fire and his dog....

I guess more drastic measures will need to be taken. I never thought that things could get this far out of hand."

"I know just the right people to handle it. For the right price they will take care of everything ... and insure that it can't be traced back to us."

"Do what you have to do. The rest of us will back you."

Chapter 25

Evansville, N.C.—November 18, 2005

"Dr. Davidson, this is Dr. Susan Aldrich at the State Medical Board. I understand you are Chief of Surgery at Midsouth Regional Medical Center."

"Yes.

I know who you are Dr. Aldrich. I'm familiar with your work on the board. How can I help you?"

"I've been looking into some complaints about one of your surgeons there ... a Dr. David Fortner. What can you tell me about him?"

"He's our gallbladder man ... at least, that's what he mostly does. What exactly are you investigating?"

She shared one of the letters with him. He in turn discussed his findings to that point.

"This could represent something serious. I think I'd better plan a trip down there very soon to check things out. I'll call Dr. Smithson and schedule a visit.

Thanks for your help. I'll arrange for us to meet when I get there."

* * * *

Evansville, N.C.—November 21, 2005

Despite having spent most of the weekend in surgery, and several hours the evening before in medical records working on the Fortner matter, Jack was up at his usual hour.

He took his usual early morning walk, had a cup of coffee and then showered. The day promised to be full, with early morning surgery followed by a busy day in the office.

He had another cup of coffee, the second in a long succession of cups that he would consume on an average day. Lynn was up earlier than usual ... she had a lot on her mind.

"Can I fix you something to eat, Jack? I'm sure you didn't get much yesterday."

Jack usually snacked in the surgeon's lounge at the hospital, but this morning the offer sounded good.

"How about a bagel with some butter, peanut butter and jelly?"

She already had them waiting, and popped two into the toaster.

"You're always one step ahead of me", he retorted.

"Now, tell me about what you found in medical records last night that was so interesting", she said as he took a big bite of his bagel and chased it with coffee.

He summarized his findings and his preliminary conclusions from the data.

"I'm really concerned that the large number of patients being seen by the same set of physicians, coupled with frequent negative gallbladder studies, and ERCP exams being done for marginal reasons. It has to be more than a coincidence.

I don't think it's conclusive proof just yet ... but something just doesn't feel right about it." He confided in her the substance of the phone call from Dr. Aldrich the previous week.

"And now I've got even more data to share with her.

This would certainly be one huge scandal if we can prove what we think is going on here is real. It has to be for financial gain ... I mean why else would they be performing all these apparently bogus procedures?

What I really don't understand is how *these* particular people could be involved together? I'm not aware that they work or socialize together any more than anyone else at the hospital.

I presume Dave Fortner is the ringleader ... he certainly would appear to have the most to gain financially. And God knows he appears to need more money than just about anyone else ever since he married Sarah Coleman."

"Jack, promise me that whatever you do to investigate the matter, that you'll be extra careful.

Things are clearly out of control already ... I mean the office, and then **Bonkers**. I really think you should talk to Captain Leonard before you do anything else."

There was genuine fright in the tenor of her voice.

"You know I'm always careful", he said, trying to reassure her.

"But I need more concrete information before going to the police. Then I'll talk to the Captain again.

Dr. Aldrich from the state medical board should be here in a few days as well. She'll know how to handle this kind of matter without tipping our hands prematurely.

I also have an obligation to share it with the Executive Committee and with Bill Smithson before taking it outside the medical center. They need to know that we suspect something illegal is going on within their walls.

Now, I'd better get going. I have an endoscopy and several surgeries this morning and I need to make rounds first."

He kissed her and was off to the hospital.

*   *   *   *

Shortly after leaving the house, Jack had an uneasy feeling that he was being followed. He wasn't sure, although he couldn't help but notice the Volvo sedan that seemed to shadow his every turn.

"It must be my imagination playing with my brain. I've been watching too many spy movies."

After a few more blocks and several turns, the car was still there. A coincidence ... or was someone really following him?

He decided to do what he had always seen them do in movies: make a few unusual turns and follow that with a u-turn and see what the other vehicle does in response.

He had just concluded the u-turn portion of his maneuvers when he saw that the Volvo continued straight down the street in the opposite direction.

"Ah! It was just my imagination after all", he concluded.

He made a turn into the next side street, pleased that the car was no longer behind him, and thinking about his next move in the Fortner affair. While those thoughts held his concentration, he failed to see the large dump truck that had pulled into the center of the street a short distance from the corner.

By the time he caught a glimpse of it from the corner of his eye, it was too late to avoid a collision. He hit his brakes as hard as he could and swerved to one side ... but to no avail. The car careened out of control as the brakes locked, sending the vehicle up under the rear of the truck. The front end of Jack's car was now nestled up under the truck's high rear bumper. The dashboard and steering column had been forced back against the front seat, wedging Jack between the two.

Passersby in cars, and pedestrians nearby responded to the sound of screeching brakes and twisting metal and breaking glass with horror, thinking it impossible for anyone to survive the accident judging from what they had heard and the carnage they had witnessed.

Within minutes, police and EMS units were scrambling in response to a ***911*** call placed by one of the witnesses.

Jack lay in the front seat pinned in by the twisted steering column. He had blood and broken glass all over his body ... and he lay motionless. The police didn't know whether he was in a coma ... or dead. He had a large gash across his forehead from the impact.

"He looks like a goner," said the officer to the first EMS crew that arrived.

"Can you feel a pulse?"

The EMS crew surveyed his body for signs of life.

"He has a weak pulse ... but at least it's there. He's not breathing well. It looks like he could have some broken ribs."

The EMS personnel performed their assessment routine including inserting an oral airway to assist in breathing while they began the extrication process from the badly mangled car. They started an IV and splinted his neck and deformed leg before placing him on a spine board for transport after having employed the ***Jaws of Life*** to free him from the damaged vehicle.

They were eight minutes from the hospital ... Midsouth. They radioed ahead, giving a report on his condition and requesting any additional orders from the physician on duty.

If he was going to survive, he would need all the expert help that he could get ... and quickly.

* * * *

Bill's private line rang once again. His rectal sphincter muscles tightened and his stomach churned as he reached for the phone.

"It's done", said the voice.

"How?"

"We arranged a little accident for the doc. We got him distracted by following him and then he turned right into a side street where we had a truck waiting. He ran right into it ... probably never knew what hit him."

"Are you sure he's ... dead?"

"Hey! We're professionals, aren't we? We always deliver on what we're paid to do.

Now, about the rest of the cash?"

"It will be deposited into your private account later today ... after I'm sure he's dead. After that, our dealings are finished, and I don't ever want to hear from you again. Is that clear?"

"Absolutely. Of course, if you ever need to arrange another accident, you know who to call."

The phone clicked on the other end.

Bill's heartburn worsened by the minute.

* * * *

His intercom beeped while he sat contemplating the news from the private call. Martha indicated that Frank Li was on the phone.

"Bill ... bad news. They're bringing Jack Davidson into the E.R. He's been in a serious auto accident ... it sounds bad from the EMS call-in report, but he is *alive*."

"What are you going to do about that?" he screamed into the phone.

"What would you expect me to do ... except *my job*?"

Bill suddenly realized that Frank was out of the loop in regard to the accident.

"Of course. Forgive me for yelling. Do whatever it takes to save one of our best. I'll be over shortly. Let me know if there's anything I can do to help."

He popped several Tums into his mouth while trying to decide his next move.

* * * *

Frank Li personally placed a call to Lynn, immediately after the EMS radioed in. She was devastated by the news ... although not entirely surprised, but she had the presence of mind to specify the physicians that she wanted to care for her husband, as well as the ones that she *did not*.

She knew how stubborn Jack could be, and what a crusader he was ... and that's what she loved about him. But what would she do if she lost him? She shuddered at the thought as she made her way to the hospital.

* * * *

The web had been spun, and continued to encompass more people. And now the center was beginning to unravel. The ***denouement*** was at hand. Events were in motion that had no means of recall.

The spinner of the years could see that the end was near, and time would help unravel the final mysteries. The players would be exposed ... and their thoughts and words and deeds would be revealed for all to see ... and hear ... and judge.

Soon all would come to understand.

Revenge is an unkind word, though sometimes necessary ... and sometimes justified.

Chapter 26

▼

Midsouth—November 21, 2005

Jack and Lynn had discussed the possibility of an emergency medical situation occurring sometime in their respective lives, and who they would prefer to have taking care of them in that unlikely event. So it was comforting for her to know that these special people were available and en route to the hospital in Jack's most desperate time of need.

EMS personnel had found it necessary to intubate Jack en route to the E.R., as his respiratory function had deteriorated. He was immediately placed on a respirator in the trauma room while the full extent of his injuries were being assessed.

He had sustained serious head, neck, and chest injuries at a minimum when his car struck and ran under the parked truck. His body lay bundled up in the usual EMS paraphernalia: neck brace and spinal immobilization board, while IV fluids were running wide open through large bore IV lines in each forearm. In addition, he had a still larger line inserted into his superior vena cava through a neck vein as soon as he arrived at the hospital emergency room.

The trauma response team members that had been alerted as soon as the ambulance called in the report were there to assess Jack when he arrived, despite having been at offices or other hospital duties when they got the news of his urgent situation.

Darwin Heller, the neurosurgeon, Ben Thomas, the general/thoracic surgeon, and Jim Akins, the orthopedic surgeon were joined by a host of hospital personnel including lab and x-ray techs, respiratory therapists and E.R. nurses.

Frank Li was the E.R. physician in charge. But with the entourage of specialists already on hand, he had essentially been pushed aside and forced to yield to their expertise. He would be ***helpless to do anything*** for his good friend.

The evaluation of Jack's injuries proceeded in an orderly, albeit rapid fashion, mandatory in such situations. Ben Thomas took charge, the general surgeon being the designated team leader in cases of multiple trauma.

Neck x-rays failed to show any fractures or dislocations, so it was safe to move Jack as necessary to perform other tests. Blood and urine samples were obtained; a chest x-ray was taken to check for evidence of broken ribs or damaged or collapsed lungs. Blood gases were measured to determine Jack's ability to deliver life-sustaining oxygen to his body tissues. Blood counts were taken to measure blood loss and blood chemistries for evidence of disruption of other necessary elements in the blood stream. A sample was used to cross-match blood for transfusions that would undoubtedly be necessary to save his life.

In fact, the team deemed it necessary to transfuse him right away, using unmatched O-negative blood until the fully cross-matched blood was available. Fortunately, Jack was O+ ... the commonest blood type. O-negative is considered the universal donor blood type since it lacks major antibodies to the other blood types.

"His left femur is broken", said Jim.

"We'll stabilize it for now with traction, but we'll need additional x-rays and possibly an arteriogram later. His foot pulse is a little weak ... he may have injured his popliteal artery."

"His right pupil is enlarged and sluggishly reacting, and he's showing some decerebrate posturing as well", said Darwin.

"We'll need a CAT scan of his head ... he probably has a skull fracture with some bleeding.

How about you, Ben?"

"His chest x-ray shows a little haziness and his mediastinum is a little wide ... so we'll need a CAT scan of his chest as well. I wouldn't want to miss an aortic injury. I don't see any rib fractures or pneumothorax on his plain chest x-ray.

I'm going to do a quick belly tap ... if it's grossly bloody, I'll just explore him. If it's negative, we'll add a CAT scan of his belly to the list. Right now, he needs more blood and fluids ... his pressure is low."

"What's our pressure now?" Ben shouted to the E.R. nurse in charge.

"About 80/60. His pulse is 130. But their both staying pretty steady so far", replied the nurse.

The belly tap showed only a tinge of bloody fluid, so Ben added a CAT scan of the abdomen to the list.

"Keep that blood going in fast", shouted Ben.

"Now, let's get him to x-ray."

* * * *

Members of the trauma team know their jobs and perform them quickly and efficiently without being prompted by others. And so, Jack Davidson, surgeon, usually a member of that life-saving team, now lay on the unfamiliar recipient side ... counting on the team that he was so familiar with ... and frequently led ... to bring him through the greatest crisis of his life.

* * * *

"The CAT scanner is ready", shouted one of the x-ray techs to the group. The E.R. nurse in charge led the procession escorting Jack's broken body to the scanner room.

"We've added an abdomen on", said Ben to the tech.

"Start with the head first."

In this new age of technology, many answers are obtained in a matter of minutes with CAT scans and MRI's. Years ago, many similar situations would have prompted a watch and wait game ... or often unnecessary surgery ... to obtain the same information.

And too often, the results were fatal no matter which way the game was played. But today, instant results allowed appropriate action to be instituted immediately.

Ten minutes had gone by ... fifteen minutes ... and the scanner was completing the exams as developed images began exiting the processor.

"We've got a subdural hematoma in the right parietal area along with a linear skull fracture ... I'll need to drain the hematoma immediately", said Darwin.

"The rest of the brain looks o.k. I'll notify the O.R. that we'll be up as soon as you check the other films", he said to Ben.

"Let me know what you'll need to do and I'll relay the message to the O.R. so that they can have everything we'll need ready to go."

"We'll know in just a few minutes", added Jim.

"I'm going to have them scan the knee for possible vascular injury; if it's OK, I don't think we'll need an arteriogram. We can just put an external splint on the leg and rod it later when he's stable."

"Damn", said Ben as he viewed the abdominal CAT scan films.

"He's got a busted spleen. He'll need a laparotomy ... that'll give me a chance to check everything else while I'm removing it. The good news is ... if there is such a thing here ... the chest looks OK."

Meanwhile, Lynn had arrived at the hospital and was brought to the OR family waiting area to talk to the three surgeons.

"Lynn", Ben led off. He sat down beside her and took her hand as he spoke.

"Jack has been badly injured in a collision with a truck, but we think he can pull through. We need to operate right away. I'll need to remove his spleen and check for any other intraabdominal injuries.

But most importantly, Darwin needs to drain a subdural hematoma." He turned to Darwin for further clarification.

"We need to drain the hematoma and elevate a slightly depressed skull fracture. That will relieve the pressure on his brain. Right now, he's decerebrate ... so hopefully that will allow him to make a complete recovery. But you know it will be a watch and wait situation afterward."

"And I'm going to stabilize a femur fracture. I'll need to insert a rod later ... but for now we don't want to keep him in surgery any longer than we have to", added Jim.

Their collective comments were overwhelming. But Lynn was a nurse and understood the urgency of the situation, and the need for immediate action despite the risks.

"Will he make it?"

The words were barely audible as they exited her lips. Tears were welling up in the corner of each eye.

"Jack's tough and we're going to do everything we can." They stopped short of suggesting any guarantee of success.

"He has faith in all three of you ... and so do I. That's why we chose you to take care of him ... or me ... in case something like this ..." Tears finished the sentence for her.

"The O.R. is ready" came the word from the head nurse.

"We'll be back out to talk to you as soon as we can", Ben said to Lynn, still holding her hand.

She forced a smile.

"You do whatever is necessary to save Jack. You have my permission to do everything you can."

She gave each of them a hug.

The entourage departed the Radiology area by the special elevator to the O.R. suite.

* * * *

Frank Li made his way to the lounge where Lynn had gone to await news of Jack's condition.

"Lynn, I'm so sorry to hear about Jack." Sitting down beside her, he embraced her.

"I know that Jack will be just fine. He's a tough guy ... and besides, you've got all the best people in the world taking care of him.

I just called Cindy and asked her to come over and stay with you while Jack's in surgery.

Is there anything else I can do to help? I'm afraid I have to get back to work. The E.R. has been terribly busy today."

"Thanks. You two have been such good friends over the years. Just knowing that you're here and willing to help is a great comfort to me.

Oh Frank!

He's got to make it!" She let loose another flood of tears and put her head on his shoulder.

"I'm sure he'll pull through", he said in low tones, trying to reassure himself as well as Lynn.

"What about the children ... have they been notified?"

"No. I need to call Jack, Jr. at college. And the other two need to be picked up from school."

"Let me get Cindy to do that for you when she gets here. You call Jack, Jr. and arrange for him to get home."

"That would be a great help.

Now I just need to decide how and what to tell the children about their Dad."

She sat back down and waited for Cindy to join her.

* * * *

"Hi, it's Frank.

They all think that he can survive the injuries. Are you still coming down? Lynn is here."

"I'll be there shortly."

The line went dead.

"Damn! This is a day that I feared might come.
He'd better have some permanent brain damage or we're all screwed."
He reached into the drawer for more Tums.

* * * *

Things in O.R. 3 were ready to go as soon as the trio arrived. More blood had been requisitioned and was being transfused. Tubes had been placed into Jack's stomach and urinary bladder in the E.R. He had been intubated en route to the hospital and on a respirator since his arrival. Intravenous antibiotics had been given right after admission. So there was nothing left to do but prep the operative sites and begin the surgery.

Ben and Darwin began simultaneously, each needing to arrest the bleeding occurring in their respective operative sites. Bleeding into the subdural space can be deadly or seriously damaging to the brain if not stopped and the pressure from the accumulated blood relieved.

And bleeding into the abdominal cavity from a ruptured spleen can lead to irreversible shock if not stopped in a timely fashion, usually by removing the damaged organ.

And Ben needed to make sure that it was the only source of intraabdominal bleeding.

"I've got the spleen controlled", said Ben, after only a few minutes inside Jack's abdomen. He quickly moved to check for other injuries.

"There's some mesenteric hematoma, but that should be OK. His liver looks fine. The pancreas and kidneys appear uninjured. I'm going to run the gut ... if that's normal, then we'll irrigate everything and I'll be ready to close.

How are you coming, Darwin?"

"I've got the small fracture elevated, and I'm just now opening the dura to drain the hematoma. With any luck, I'll be finished in about ten minutes."

Ben finished his work quickly. As he began to close the abdominal incision, he suggested to Jim that he proceed with the fracture stabilization.

"I can help you in a minute if you need an assistant", Ben indicated to Jim.

"Thanks, but this really won't take long.

Besides, I've already got good help", he said, referring to the O.R. tech standing next to him.

"How are things at the head of the table?" Ben said to Ken Boniface, the anesthesiologist.

"Leveling off nicely, now that you two have the bleeding controlled and the pressure relieved from the brain."

Darwin was just finishing draining the hematoma.

"Blood pressure is now 110/60 and pulse 100. His O2 (oxygen) saturation is 100%. We're hyperventilating him at Darwin's request to lower his pCO2 (carbon dioxide) and help reduce brain swelling. We'll keep him paralyzed and on the respirator until we know how he's going to respond.

We've got Mannitol running too. His urine output has been a little slow, but it's starting to pick up since his pressure has stabilized. I've given him four units of packed cells, so I'm rechecking his blood count now to see if he needs any more."

Darwin had just finished closing the skull defect.

'Now, if he doesn't have too bad a concussion, he may just be all right."

As soon as Jim finished, dressings were applied and Jack was readied for the trip to his room in the Intensive Care Unit.

*   *   *   *

Within ten minutes of completion of the multiple surgical procedures, the parade of people escorting the bed carrying Jack Davidson was en route to the second floor I.C.U. Doctors, nurses, O.R. personnel and respiratory techs all made their way, with Jack the focus of their attention.

Elaine and Sharon had volunteered for extra duty when they heard that their favorite surgeon would be coming to the unit as a patient. They wanted to assure Lynn that he got the best possible care ... and be close should something untoward occur.

CHAPTER 27

▼

Midsouth—November 22, 2005

Twenty-four long hours had elapsed since the accident that could have instantly claimed Jack's life ... and might yet do so. Still his vital signs were stable; there was no evidence of any further bleeding, and his leg fracture was in good alignment.

But he remained in a coma.

His breathing was mechanical, performed by a machine. The waiting game to determine the final outcome was well underway.

A follow up head CAT scan the following morning showed minimal contusion with only mild edema. The hematoma had not re-accumulated. So there were no real surprises. While this should have represented good news to the doctors and to Jack's family, only his awakening would give them the satisfaction they sought.

Darwin Hiller was cautiously optimistic that Jack's condition would improve based upon the clinical findings and radiological test results. But then he was a friend and colleague.

And doctors know that colleagues don't always follow the rulebook when it comes to making full recoveries, in spite of everyone's best wishes and efforts ... and prayers.

Cindy Li had brought the children from school the afternoon before, and Jack, Jr. had made it home by that evening and joined them at the hospital ... where they had all kept an overnight vigil.

They offered each other the strength to endure these desperate times. Jack and Lynn had taught the children the importance of family as they grew.

"Your family is the most important relationship you will have in your entire lifetime. Always stay in touch with your brothers and sisters and your parents. Cherish them and trust them and know that in times of need they will be there for you.

Friends come and friends go, but your family is forever!

One of your father's favorite quotations is from a poem by Robert Frost: ***The Death of the Hired Man.***" Tears fell from her eyes at the utterance of the word ***father.*** She regained her composure and continued.

"Home is the place where, when you have to go there, they have to take you in."

So the family remained close during the vigil, giving each other the support they desperately needed at this crucial juncture. They were assisted by Jack's friend, Father Phil, who led them in prayer for Jack's full and speedy recovery from his injuries.

* * * *

And still the waiting continued.

Forty-eight hours came and went ... with no detectible significant change. As they entered the third post-operative day, concerns of infection, pulmonary problems secondary to the lung contusion and prolonged intubation, and fat emboli from the long bone fracture remained the major concern. But Ben had amassed all the specialists necessary to evaluate each problem and treat them in the most appropriate way ... and prevent anything they could.

The rest remained in the hands of Jack and ***fate.*** Jack had always been a fighter. But circumstances like this are beyond one's control and the role of personal determination was questionable at best.

"Generally, the sooner one regains consciousness after a head injury, the better the prognosis." Darwin was straightforward in answering Lynn's question about Jack's ultimate prognosis. At the same time, he tried to be reassuring.

"I've seen people go days or weeks in a coma, only to awaken with little or no residual damage. I have no reason to believe that Jack can't make a full recovery based upon everything I've seen so far."

Lynn wanted to believe his words, but remained reluctant to do so.

"Are you sure ... I mean, you're not just trying to be nice ... to appease me?"

"Lynn, I'm your friend. I've known Jack for a long time. You know I'd tell you the truth no matter what. If I seriously thought we were facing a bad outcome, I'd want to tell you to help prepare you and your family for the worst.

I know it's not easy to sit and wait like this, but try to be patient. It took me a number of years after my residency to develop the necessary patience for the specialty I'm in. It would be hard to do my job if I stayed in a state of chronic anxiety."

"Thank you, Darwin. You've been a good friend. I know that Jack appreciates all that you're doing for him, as I do." She reached over and gave him a hug.

Lynn valued the manner in which everyone had gone out of their way to be kind and encouraging to her with their comments. She asked to speak with Sharon and Elaine.

"He's so fond of you two. He's shared so many stories of your dedication to him and his patients over the years. I just want you to know that I appreciate the care you've each given him, and I know if there is a chance for him to recover, it will have been due in large part to the wonderful care that you've provided."

They sat in the nurses' lounge for a while longer, sharing stories and a few more tears. Finally, at the nurses' insistence, Lynn gathered up the family and headed home for some much needed rest.

* * * *

Cindy Li stopped by the house. She had visited Lynn several times at the hospital after bringing the children there from school the day of the accident.

"I hope I'm not intruding."

"Cindy, you're always welcome here ... especially now when I need someone my own age to talk to.

The children know that their father is seriously ill, and we've discussed the possibility that he might not make it, or be seriously impaired from the head injury ... but somehow the potential finality of it all doesn't fully register with them.

And I guess in a sense that's just as well."

"I know how it was in my family when my mother was ill. People always assume that someone will automatically get better ... but she had advanced cancer and died.

It's only then that they realize that finality you've been talking about.

Anyway, Frank and I just wanted you to know that we're thinking about you, and praying for Jack's recovery.

I was heading to the grocery store, and thought you might want to go with me, or let me get something you might need if you'd rather not go right now."

"That's kind of you, Cindy.

In fact, I do need some things and it might do me good to get out of the house for a few minutes. I've got my cell phone if anyone needs to reach me. Jack, Jr. can watch the other two."

* * * *

Elaine nudged Sharon.

"Have you noticed how often Dr. Fortner has been stopping by to check on Dr. Davidson's progress?

I know that they occasionally help each other with surgical cases, but I never got the impression that they were particularly good friends. Other staff members are not so obvious about their visits.

He's asked me several times to update him on his condition. He knows that I can't be too specific since he's not one of the doctors caring for him.

He keeps wanting to know 'if he's going to make it'."

Sharon replied in her usual charitable way.

"Maybe he's just wondering what it would be like if the situation were reversed and he was the one in the coma ... wondering ... hoping that friends and staff members would be as concerned about his progress as they are about Dr. Davidson's."

"Still, I'm curious about his motive" Elaine countered. Annette and Bobbi, two of the other nurses on duty, had overheard the conversation and joined in.

"You know, when I started working here I thought that Dr. Fortner was a neat guy. He was friendly ... he'd stop by and have coffee with us and kid around. He'd tell us about flying his plane and some of the harrowing experiences that he'd had. He even asked me to go up with him once.

That was when Sarah Coleman was working here. After they met, he began to change. And after they were married ... well, he's never been the same. Now it's just work, work, work. He seems to have less time for his patients, and no time for socializing with us."

"So, you all have noticed it too," said Elaine.

"Her spending habits are what keeps him working all the time, according to what I hear. She must really have **something special** for him to put up with her." She rolled her eyes as she spoke.

"I never cared for her when she worked here, and even less when she became Director of Patient Care. I certainly wasn't upset when she announced her resignation."

There was a hint of jealousy in all their comments. It was clear that the conversation had degenerated into a gossip session.

And while they gossiped, Dave Fortner had come and gone once again from the I.C.U.

*   *   *   *

Midsouth—November 16, 2005

Mike Herman had finally completed his work on the Roddenberry autopsy, and was preparing to release his official report. The hospital, doctors, family, N.C. state medical board, insurance companies ... all were awaiting his conclusions.

The report was lengthy, chronicling in detail all the medical and pathologic data pertinent to the findings. But it was the conclusion that they all were focused on.

"Upon review of all the pre- and post-mortem data, it is the conclusion of this examiner that the patient, Alice Roddenberry:

1. Suffered from cholecystitis and choledocholithiasis (stones in the common bile duct); and that the procedure being performed at the time of death (ERCP) was appropriate.
2. Death is attributed to an idiosyncratic form of angioedema associated with the ingestion of a drug, Captopril, taken by the patient on the morning of her death. It was not reported to any medical or nursing personnel by the patient or family on routine pre-procedure screening.
3. The relationship between angioedema and Captopril is extremely rare and would not have been cause for cancellation of the procedure even had it been known in advance.
4. Proper resuscitation maneuvers were performed in an attempt to save the life of the deceased, but were inadequate due to severe airway obstruction.
5. Death was unavoidable.

*   *   *   *

Each of the interested parties was sent a copy of the official report and now had the option to accept or challenge the opinion of Dr. Michael Herman, Chief of Hematology and Blood-banking, Department of Pathology, Midsouth Regional Medical Center.

Chapter 28

Midsouth—November 22, 2005

By now, Bill was taking his Zantac twice daily and supplementing it with Tums and Rolaids ... his "life-savers", as he called them. He also kept a bottle of liquid Maalox in his desk drawer and in his nightstand at home ... just in case. His stomach was not handling the increasing stress well at all. And things were fast approaching a fever pitch.

He had visited Lynn several times since the accident to console and encourage her ... and he was being kept completely up to date on Jack's condition.

Martha beeped him on his intercom.

"Your son, Bill, is on the phone for you."

He was momentarily relieved, anticipating a pleasant diversion. But the respite was brief. After the usual pleasantries and family enquiries, Bill, Jr. got to the real purpose of his call.

"Dad, I need to talk to you on a professional level. There are some problems concerning several members of your medical staff there at Midsouth that I have agreed to investigate. I've read some preliminary data ... and it appears that there could be a serious problem going on.

Please don't discuss this with anyone. I need to come to Evansville to discuss the matter with you. Would Friday morning be o.k.? We could discuss it over breakfast."

Bill could only suspect what the nature of the enquiry was, and he knew he couldn't put Bill, Jr. off indefinitely.

"Friday is not good for me. You know, it's Thanksgiving week and the hospital will be essentially on a holiday routine.

How about next Monday morning?"

That would give Bill the whole weekend to investigate things and plot strategy.
"You're right. I was forgetting about the holiday.
That will be fine. I'll see you around eight-thirty a.m. next Monday morning."
"Son, can you at least give me a hint what this is all about?"
"Sorry, Dad. I can't say anything over the phone. We need to discuss it face to face ... in total privacy."

The phone disconnected, leaving Bill sitting there with a stunned look on his face and a dial tone ringing in his ear.

He was afraid to hang up the phone for fear that it would ring again with more bad news.

His stomach couldn't handle that right now!

* * * *

At the Fortner house, things had not been going well for some time. For months, Dave had been nothing but a slave to Sarah ... working at a fever pace to keep up with her spending. His personal time had been cut to shreds, leaving him less and less time for flying, the one thing that gave him a reprieve from the constant harassment of his home life.

He had become noticeably more irascible to Sarah. He had made it obvious, even to her, that he preferred she not accompany him when he went flying his plane. She had done everything she could to assuage his growing anger toward her. The sexual enticement that had worked for so long, no longer held its magic for him. The events that had occurred at ***Hana*** ... the same events that had held him prisoner to her for this long year ... now meant little. The threats no longer intimidated him.

"I don't think that I can continue this charade any longer, Sarah. I'm working too hard to keep it all going ... to maintain the lifestyle that you have designed for yourself ... not for **us.**

And now this thing with Jack. I never thought that your plan would ever involve physical violence.

I don't want to be a part of it any longer.

I can't be a part of it any longer."

Sarah walked across the bedroom, put her arms around his neck and attempted to give him a kiss.

He rebuffed her.

"Why don't we lie down on the bed and discuss this a little more?"

From the tone of his voice and his body language, she knew that she had better not ignore him any longer.

"No.

Not anymore, Sarah. You think that you can just turn on your charm any time you feel like it ... entice me into the bedroom, and I'm supposed to act like any other sex-starved man and make love to you and forget what the argument was all about.

Well, it was fun while it lasted. But it can't cure the misery that life together with you has produced.

So, no more.

I've wanted to say that to you for some time now.

I wish to God that I had never asked you to go to Hawaii with me ... that I had never agreed to your little plan to see **Hana**. I wish I had never even heard that name ... **Hana**. I wish that that night had never happened."

"But it did happen, just the way I intended it.

And don't deny that you've enjoyed all the benefits of my little plan. You certainly can't deny that the sex was good.

And that plane that you love so much ... that gives you the freedom that you need ... you've been able to afford that as well.

Come on now, darling. Tell the truth."

Dave was momentarily confused. Sarah was at least partially right ... he had enjoyed the sex and the travel and his plane. But gradually things had deteriorated.

At first, he had agreed that inconveniencing a few people or taking money from a fat-cat insurance company would be o.k. And the embarrassed doctors that she lured into the plan ... well, they were probably getting their just desserts ... and anyway they had been compensated well for their efforts.

But now they had resorted to criminal activity ... and that had crossed the line.

It couldn't possibly be worth any of it when it all came to an end.

And that end appeared to be fast approaching now.

"I'm going out for a drive. I need some time to think this all through."

"May I remind you of the little surprise pictures we took that night?"

"You can take your damn pictures and publish them in the local newspaper if you like.

You can hardly ruin my life any more than you already have!"

The frustration showed on his face. For someone so used to being in control of his affairs at work, he felt that his personal life had become totally unmanageable, much like a plane that has lost its rudder, that was spiraling toward earth in a death dive.

And being a seasoned pilot, he didn't like the feeling at all.

Chapter 29

▼

Midsouth—November 26, 2005

"Where am I?
 What is this place?
 Why can't I talk?
 What am I doing in this bed?
 Wait! I'm in the hospital. I was driving a car ... someone following me ... or so I thought. I turned a corner ... then there was a large truck in the middle of the street ... couldn't avoid hitting it, even though I tried not to.
 I think I hit it ... why else would I be here? Hard to remember ... all those details. But I'm still alive ... I mean, why else would I be here in the hospital?
 It's a place for the living ... not the dead ... except briefly.
 Who is that? Oh, it's Elaine. It's no wonder they call them 'Angels of Mercy' ... nurses. She's so gentle and attentive to all my needs.
 I should know about needs. I've taken care of enough people in situations similar to mine. And she has been there so many times helping me and my patients.
 And now I'm the patient!
 Well, Elaine, how am I doing? I wonder why she has a tear in her eye every time she comes in here to do something for me? Does she know something about me that I don't know?
 Hey! What do I know ... nothing? I can't read my chart ... can't see the entries in the progress notes to indicate if I'm getting better ... or worse. I can't see the x-ray or lab reports.
 And I can't examine myself to check for signs of improvement ... or worsening.

Maybe if they took this tube out of my throat I could talk. Sure, then I couldn't breathe. They wouldn't have it in me if I didn't need it, would they?

Of course not. I've got the best people taking care of me. Lynn saw to that.

And Lynn ... the love of my life. My best friend and constant companion for over twenty years. How I miss holding her. And that sad look on her face when she comes to visit.

Lord! Let me make her feel better. She doesn't deserve this. She's had to suffer enough over the years. This profession has not always been kind. And now that the children are almost grown, give us a chance to enjoy life together before you call me.

Who's coming now? The curtain is opening ... oh, it's Dave Fortner. I wonder why he's in here so often? He's not on the list of people taking care of me. What could he possibly want? Does he know that I have been investigating him? Does he suspect something? What is it that he is saying?"

"Jack, I never knew that it would come to this. You have to understand that I didn't start this ... I'm only one of the pawns. I was blackmailed just like the others. I thought it was just for the money ... but now it's totally out of control, and I don't know what to do to stop it.

I'm not sure if I am strong enough ... I've been weak for so long. I didn't know that anyone would get hurt ... especially not you. We've never been the best of friends, but I think you know that I have always respected your surgical abilities ... and especially your integrity.

Frankly, I've always been a little jealous of your relationship with the nursing staff and our medical colleagues. Believe me, I would never have done anything like this to you myself."

"What does he mean by that ... hurt me? I thought that the accident was my fault. And who are the others he keeps referring to?

Oh God! Get me out of here!"

*   *   *   *

"Why is it that everyone always has to do what *you* want? I'm tired of being the little sister who never gets her way. Ever since we were kids, *you* were always in charge ... *you* always knew best ... *you* always controlled our every move."

"But someone had to take charge ... someone had to take care of the three of us ... and I am the oldest. If our stepmother had cared for us, she would have taken us out of that Godforsaken place.

It was my responsibility to look after the three of us ... I was the one who took most of father's punishments. Doesn't that count for something?"

Sarah liked playing the sympathy card. She knew that her statements would conjure up old memories ... and promises ... and force her sisters to recant once more.

"Not this time, **sister**.

I don't like the way you had me bring Mike into this ... forcing him to be a part of your little scheme ... making me fool him into thinking that I was pregnant so that I could force him into marrying me.

And force really wasn't necessary at all!

He *loves* me!

And all those pictures you took of us at the house in case your plan backfired ... just to get him to participate in your **project** and to get even with father, by destroying as many members of the medical profession as you could."

"Now, now, Danielle. Remember that *you* were a part of the plan all along. *You* agreed to help, and *you* set up poor old Mike. *You* were the one who got to enjoy him in bed and the one that did such a convincing job with the fake pregnancy.

I may have taught you well, but *you* played your part well ... very well."

Danielle quickly countered.

"And you always had your ace in the hole ... your trump card, those pictures of these poor men that we enticed into our lives ... threatening to use them if they ever decided to get out of line.

Blackmail is an evil word ... but it is what you do best!

Frankly, I'm amazed that you have been able to keep everyone dancing on a highwire all this time ... keeping them playing *your* game. But sooner or later, it will all come to an end.

And Dave.

Why you've kept the poor guy working like a slave since you conned him into marrying you. I will admit that your **Hana** scheme was brilliant ... but isn't it time to put an end to this need for revenge ... to say *enough* to your own selfish personal needs?

And now I hear that Dr. Davidson is fighting for his life in the hospital. Are you involved in that too?"

Sarah withdrew at the mention of the name. She dared not answer for fear of revealing the truth.

"My God! You are involved, aren't you?

I know that look on your face ... you can't fool me after all these years. Just what did he do to incur your wrath?"

Sarah slid over to Danielle's chair, sat down on the arm, and took her hand. Danielle reluctantly let her hold it.

"You have to understand that everything we've worked for was about to be undone by his meddling. He's been investigating hospital records, including Dave's. You even helped him with some of the x-ray reports."

"Yes, but Russ was careful to pick out mostly legitimate cases."

"But, my little sister, he's no dummy. As you told me, Mike just happened to run into him at the hospital the other night and found him looking at medical records ... mostly *project* patients. He was getting too close.

And after we had already warned him."

"Now don't tell me that the office fire was your doing too?"

"We had to do something to discourage him from looking any farther. He appeared close to figuring out what was going on. Any sane person would have taken the hint.

We only wanted to scare him away.

But I guess we underestimated Jack Davidson."

Danielle was enraged.

"Well, I've really got to hand it to you. This must be a new low ... even for you.

I'm leaving ... I need time to think about all this and decide what to do next. Look what it has done to our lives so far ... and God knows what's in store for our futures.

One thing's for sure: it can't be anything good."

"Now don't do anything rash, Danielle. You call me before you decide to do anything that we might regret.

Big *sister* still knows best!"

Danielle exited with a loud slam of the door. Sarah was momentarily stunned by her decidedly uncharacteristic behavior.

"She'll come around. She just needs to remember the past and all that I've done for her. She'll call me when she settles down."

Chapter 30

▼

Midsouth—November 28, 2005

"Dad, it's good to see you", Bill, Jr. said, extending his hand toward his father.

Bill shook it somewhat tentatively.

"Can we talk privately?"

"Of course.

Martha, we're not to be disturbed," he said to his secretary as the pair entered his private office.

Bill closed the door.

"Now, son, what is this all about? You sounded so ominous over the phone."

"Dad, this is a potentially very serious matter and I need to know that you will keep it in your strictest confidence."

"Certainly, son. You have my word.

Now, what's this all about?"

"I was asked by a friend of mine here in town to review some information given him by two women ... former patients here at Midsouth, who are alleging that they may be victims of some type of fraudulent care scheme. They are backed by a number of others who have had similar experiences ... others who are willing to become involved in legal action if facts are found to substantiate their cases.

I have already reviewed some records from both the hospital and selected physician's offices, and what I have found would seem to validate their claims.

The same physicians are involved in virtually every case: Dr. Frank Li, from your emergency department; Dr. Carl Hauser, a family practitioner; Dr. Kevin Bledsoe, a gastroenterologist; and Dr. David Fortner, the surgeon who operated on all of them.

The majority of patients had no complication ... that's not the issue. Their concern is the lack of, or very minimal symptoms that they all started with, and the procedures that they eventually endured. Almost all of them had a procedure called an ERCP done by this Dr. Bledsoe prior to their surgery ... and they are not sure why. Most of them got seriously ill *only after* having the procedure done, and that's when they were referred for surgery.

Most are concerned as well about the disparity of the test results reported to them by the various physicians involved. We think that some of these procedures ... especially the ERCP, and possibly the surgery ... did not need to be done.

Dad, I need to know that I can count on your cooperation in investigating the matter further. There are additional hospital records, lab work and x-ray studies that will need to be released and reviewed."

Bill paused before speaking, acting as though the allegations came as a total shock.

"Wow!

Son, those are some powerful accusations that you are throwing around. I know that you understand the implications of what you are saying, and I know that you will be careful in your investigation.

You know that you will need to talk to the Medical Staff Executive Committee since this will involve getting permission both from patients and physicians."

"In due time, Dad. Right now, I'd like as few people as possible to know what's going on. I might inadvertently play into the wrong hands, since we don't know who else may be involved. Perhaps I could just speak with the Chief-of-Staff."

"That's a smart move. He can represent the committee for now. I can have Martha see if he's available while we go for breakfast.

Any way, it's wonderful to know that I raised a son with a good head on his shoulders." Bill patted his son on the back as they proceeded to the outer office.

Martha informed Bill that the Chief of Staff would be out of town for two weeks, and that the Vice Chief, Dr. Russ Callahan was available.

"Let me step back into my office and make a quick phone call," said Bill, Sr.

"Then I promise we'll get something to eat. You must be starving after getting up so early and driving all the way here from Raleigh."

Bill disappeared back into his private office and quickly dialed the direct number into Russ's office. Fortunately, he answered the phone.

"Russ, it's all coming apart," he said in panicked tones. He explained the situation and Bill, Jr's need to talk to him.

"I think that we need to get the whole group together and develop a strategy for handling this ... to see if it's salvageable ... and to decide what you should tell him when you talk to him. In the meantime, I'll stall him and try to put off any serious talking until tomorrow."

"O.K., Bill" replied Russ.

"What am I ever going to tell my family when this all comes unhinged? How can I ever explain this to Maggie, or the children ... especially Bill, Jr?"

He grabbed some Rolaids from the drawer as he hurried back out to meet his son in the outer office.

* * * *

Midsouth—November 27, 2005

For six days and nights following his accident and the surgery that followed, Jack lay in a coma in the I.C.U. at Midsouth. His vital signs had stabilized. His lungs remained clear with the help of vigorous pulmonary toilet. There was no indication of sepsis. His laboratory tests were either normal or improving. He had passed the critical time period for serious sequelae of brain swelling.

But, he remained unresponsive!

Elaine was in Jack's cubicle performing some routine duties, when she suddenly let out a shout for Sharon to come.

"I think he's waking up" she squealed enthusiastically.

"I know that I just saw his hand move and his eye blink."

"I'll put in a call to Dr. Hiller. You watch and tell me if you see him move. Dr. Hiller wanted to be notified the instant we noticed anything positive ... even on his day off."

Darwin was at home, having just returned from Sunday morning church services, but immediately left for the hospital to examine Jack. By the time he arrived there, he found that his pupils were sluggish *but* responsive, and that he had a weak *but* perceptible grasp in both hands.

The trio watched him together for about thirty minutes and observed several episodes of eyelid movement.

"I think he's going to be O.K.," Darwin pronounced authoritatively.

"You ladies have done a hell of a good job as always. I'm going to call Mrs. Davidson and give her the good news right away."

* * * *

Lynn had been dressing for her first visit of the day to the hospital when the good news came from Darwin. She had almost decided that she might never hear the words "waking up". For as much as she loved her husband and his fighting spirit, she had had to be realistic about his chances for recovery ... full or otherwise. Hopefully, the next few days would provide additional answers about his ultimate outcome.

Trucks don't much care one way or the other about people and their hopes and plans, or their families, or their fighting spirit. They are usually the undisputed winners in collisions with other vehicles.

In truth, Lynn cherished her moments alone with Jack at the hospital. It afforded her the opportunity to reminisce about all the good times they had shared together over the years ... and occasional bad times. Every marriage has some of both, and the infrequent bad times made the good times even better. More than once, a tear streamed down her cheek as she relived precious moments of their years together.

She was glad that the children didn't see these moments of "weakness"; her proud German heritage demanded more outward toughness, although many's the time she would have preferred to let loose her emotions and accept the consolation of friends and family, no matter how it appeared to them.

* * * *

The next twenty-four hours more than made up for the preceding seven days. Jack had suddenly and fully awakened as if touched by the wand of an omnipotent magician ... or the hand of God. He threatened to remove his endotracheal tube ... if someone didn't do it for him. He was not about to lay there speechless. He was not going to be relegated to the cadre of "magic slate" users ... a dime-store toy used for writing and easy erasing by patients unable to talk.

Following a few quick tests to determine Jack's ability to breathe on his own, the tube was removed uneventfully. His memory of the events leading up to his accident were clouded, but gradually began to clear over the ensuing week.

"Just how close did I come to 'checking out'?" he asked Darwin while they were alone.

"Well, I don't think that anyone looked at coffins ... but close enough for the last rites. Your friend Father Phil did the honors. I'm sure that his intercession helped."

Jack drifted off to sleep while Darwin continued to drone on. How many times had he cared for people in similar circumstances? He had often wondered what it would be like to wake up and find out that you had almost died ... and unable to remember what had happened.

Perhaps that was for the best.

He awakened a short time later only to find that Darwin had left and Lynn was back beside him, holding his hand. He smiled at her and squeezed her hand. How lucky to have someone nearby that you love so much!

* * * *

Midsouth—November 30, 2005

At the perimeter of the I.C.U., a plainclothes detective from the Evansville Police Department stood talking inconspicuously with a uniformed officer stationed near Jack's cubicle.

Jack had been placed under round the clock surveillance by order of Captain Leonard. The office fire had clearly been arson; and that had been followed closely by this obvious attempt on his life. He was not about to let someone have a third crack at him ... not on his watch.

Jack had had second thoughts on the way to the hospital that morning, and had called Captain Leonard and reported **Bonker's** death and briefed him about the ongoing investigation at the hospital.

Captain Leonard had immediately dispatched cars to follow him to the hospital. However, the chase car had momentarily lost him when Jack made the sudden u-turn and subsequent detour onto a side street that resulted in his collision with the truck.

With Jack now awake, the Captain arranged a visit in the I.C.U. Jack saw the uniformed officer salute him as he entered. He continued to watch as the nurses checked the captain's I.D. and ushered him into his cubicle.

"Dr. Davidson, I'm delighted to see you doing so well. I'm sorry we weren't able to prevent the whole thing, but you didn't give us much warning that morning.

Any idea how much longer they're going to keep you in here?" referring to the I.C.U.

"Captain, I'm not entirely sure how long I've been in here, let alone how much longer they might keep me here. I'm still a bit fuzzy on just what they've done to me ... and what else they need to do.

Why do you ask?"

"Doc, I don't want to overstay my welcome, so let me get right to the point.

Your accident was no ***accident***. The truck you hit was planted there by a gang we know was hired. You were being tailed ... and they essentially enticed you there.

They were out to kill you!

Now I'm not exactly sure what this investigation you've been conducting has to do with all this. But let's assume that if there are medical people involved, and if your being alive is that important to protecting the secrecy of whatever it is they are doing, they will probably try to kill you again. And what better place to have you than right here under their noses.

We need to get you to a safer location ... a private room, where we can control the entrance and exits better than this place. There are too many people coming and going in here all day long.

Now that you are awake and talking, you'll be even more dangerous to them. It's even more urgent that we be able to protect you better."

"Do we really need all this fuss, Captain?"

"Doc, I know you are tired, and your brain is still a little fuzzy ... as you put it. Let me just remind you that in the past ten days you have had your office burned down, your dog murdered, and yourself almost killed. What do think, really?"

"I guess you're right. I just never thought that investigating what I assumed would turn out to be a harmless complaint would ever lead to this. At the worst, I thought someone was just trying to make a few bucks. I never imagined I was getting in the middle of something so big that someone would want to kill me over it.

I'm beginning to feel like the central character in a movie plot!"

"You doctors can be naïve. Things like this can happen in any profession, and yours is certainly no exception. So take my advice: let us handle this one from now on."

"O.K.", Jack said with an air of resignation. He realized that he was out of his league.

"But do me a favor, Captain. If there is any way that you can use me as 'bait' to catch your 'perps' ... I think that's the term you use for suspects ... don't hesitate to ask me. I think a little getting even is in order."

"I'll keep that in mind. But for now, I think I had better go and let you get some rest. I'll be checking with your doctors about that room transfer. We'll talk more later."

*   *   *   *

Midsouth—December 1, 2005

The Intensive Care Unit is a major nerve center of most major metropolitan hospitals. It is the place wherein life teeters on the brink ... where critical decisions are the norm ... and where activity is constant.

Repeated intrusions on the privacy of each patient are the daily norm. Doctors and nurses, lab and x-ray techs, and numerous paramedical personnel constantly disturb patients in the name of rendering care.

Inherent in the delivery of that care is a constant parade of people entering and exiting the unit at all times of the day and night. Nursing personnel assigned to the high traffic areas of the hospital are charged with keeping constant vigilance, evaluating and monitoring their movements much like guards in a high security compound.

The morning following Captain Leonard's visit, Elaine observed the approach of an unfamiliar lab tech, ostensibly there to obtain a blood sample from Jack Davidson. Though his credentials appeared authentic, she kept a watch on him out of the corner of her eye as he entered Jack's cubicle and placed his phlebotomy tray on the bedside table.

"Hey! What are you doing in there?" Elaine yelled as he slipped a syringe from his lab coat pocket, raised it with the needle showing and appeared to be inserting it into the I.V. injection port, obviously intending to inject whatever substance it held.

She yelled with such a voluminous tone that it scared her as well as the apparently bogus lab tech. Realizing that he had been observed, the perpetrator dropped the syringe onto the floor and ran from the room towards the back stairway at the end of the hall that led from the I.C.U.

The security guard, sensing a crime in progress, immediately gave chase, but to no avail. The perpetrator disappeared before the guard had reached the stairwell door. He immediately notified his central office of the event, gave a description of the perpetrator, and ordered the building sealed. Other guards ran to the various exits in an effort to keep the suspect in the building while they attempted to locate and apprehend him.

Elaine ran to Jack's cubicle.

"Are you all right, Dr. Davidson?"

"I think so, thanks to you. I think you caught him just in time. Another few seconds and he probably would have injected whatever was in that syringe into my I.V. I was half asleep and didn't quite realize what was happening until you screamed.

Did he get away with the syringe?"

"No. It's right here on the floor, under your bed where it rolled."

By now the security guard from the police department and the plainclothes detective were in the room.

"Just leave that there until our lab people can retrieve it. They'll want to check for prints on the surface of the syringe as well as analyze its contents."

"Elaine", said Jack, "I don't know how to thank you. You're getting real good at saving my life."

He reached for her hand as he spoke.

"I'll always be grateful for all that you've done for me."

*   *   *   *

The crime scene investigation team arrived within the hour, retrieved the syringe from under the bed with its contents intact, and briefly spoke to Jack about the event. Before they were finished, Captain Leonard appeared on the scene.

"You see what I mean, Doc? They almost got you right here in front of everyone, just like I predicted."

"I won't doubt you again, Captain", said Jack.

"Have you found the guy?"

"No. But thanks to your nurse, you, and the guard that pursued him, we have a pretty good description. Security has the building sealed off, so it's just a matter of time until we find him.

We're checking with other areas of the hospital to see if anyone recognized him. He won't get away, I promise."

* * * *

"I was spotted just as I was about to inject the 'juice' into his IV line, so the doc's still with us."

"Jesus! That's twice you've botched the job. What do you think we're paying you for?"

"Cheer up Dr. S. We'll finish the job this time ... and for free."

"You'd better, or we're all in big trouble. And don't ever call me again on this line."

"You can bet on it."

* * * *

Bill had barely hung up his private line when it rang again. Once more, he felt intense burning in his stomach and esophagus.

"I must have an ulcer by now", he thought to himself.

It was Sarah.

"Bill, what the hell is going on? I hear that Jack is still with us. And Russ is being hounded for records from your son and from the state medical board.

And Dave ... he's not himself. He's upset about Jack. Says he wants out."

"I'm sure that you can figure out a way to control him ... you are awfully good in bed, you know?"

"Thanks for the compliment ... you should know ... but, I've already tried that and it didn't work this time. He's out for a drive or up in his plane somewhere. What do you suggest that we do?"

The master was now begging the slave for help.

"I just had a call and was assured that Jack will be taken care of ... soon. Let's just sit tight for now. We can discuss it at the meeting of the group later today, and plan our strategy.

I think we'll be o.k. If we just don't panic."

"I hope you're right. Thanks for the assurance."

Bill clutched the bottle of Maalox in his right hand. After hanging up the phone, he uncapped it and drank half the bottle.

He wished that he believed the words that he had just uttered to Sarah.

"This will never work!"

Chapter 31

Evansville, N.C.—December 5, 2005

"Captain Leonard, there's a gentleman on the phone who says he needs to speak to you urgently. He won't give his name, but says it's about the Jack Davidson matter. Will you take it?"

"Of course. But put a tracer on it while we're talking. Let me pick up in my office."

"Captain Leonard, I understand that you are in charge of the Jack Davidson matter", said the unidentified caller.

"I think I can be of help to you. But you must agree to meet me alone to hear what I have to say. And since I'm involved, maybe we can make a deal if I can help you?"

"Who is this? I don't make deals with people that I don't even know." The Captain was gruff and authoritative.

"I can only tell you that I'm a part of this thing ... but I don't want to be anymore. It's gone too far ... farther than I ever thought....

If you agree to meet me privately, I'll tell you everything I know."

"You say you're a part of this?"

"Yes.

But I had nothing to do with the plans to harm anyone, especially not Jack Davidson. That's why I'm calling ... I don't want to be held responsible for any of that.

Please meet me alone in front of my office building in thirty minutes. You'll undoubtedly recognize me. You'll know that my story is legitimate when you see who I am and realize what I have to lose by volunteering to do this."

He gave him the address.

"You've got to come alone. If I see anyone else with you, the deal is off."

*   *   *   *

Captain Leonard immediately set into motion plans for the usual undercover backup unit to accompany him to the designated meeting place.

"Surely the caller must realize that a police captain is not prepared to meet an unknown person totally alone in a strange place, especially at night. And we can match people with addresses.

But then, people under stress often are not rational thinkers."

He made his way out to the police garage.

*   *   *   *

Meanwhile, Bill had had enough too. The gravity of the situation had raised his anxiety level to an all time high and the pain in his stomach was becoming more than he could tolerate. He needed to extricate himself from this worsening situation.

His options were limited to suicide or flight ... and he didn't much care for either choice.

Suicide was foreign to his religious beliefs ... if he had any left. He didn't like the suddenness and finality of it, or the stigma it would leave behind for his family. And then there was the fact that his insurance policy would not pay the several million dollars of whole life coverage in the event that he took his own life.

Fleeing to some other country gave him little time to make arrangements. The way things were unraveling, he probably had only a day or two at most.

And, if he chose that option, there could be no good-byes, no regrets, and no turning back ... he would be a marked man if he ever tired to re-enter the country.

*   *   *   *

Midsouth—December 1, 2005

Captain Leonard, in consultation with Jack's doctors, had arranged for his immediate transfer to a different room in order to afford the police protection unit better control of traffic into and out of his room.

Twenty-four hours after the second attempt on Jack's life, the contents of the syringe was identified as succinylcholine hydrochloride, a rapidly fatal and often difficult to detect muscle paralyzing drug used in anesthesia. Following its administration, breathing muscles are totally paralyzed; if the person is not intubated and placed on a respirator immediately, they would certainly be dead in a matter of minutes.

Jack, hearing the results of the analysis, shuddered to think of the fate that had almost befallen him ... and the agonizing death it would have meant ... not being able to breathe, but awake enough to know that the end was only a matter of minutes away.

"Thank God Elaine was near."

Since Jack would need additional surgery on his broken leg, a room in full view of the nurse's station on the fourth floor orthopedic ward was chosen. An anteroom for infection decontamination, connected by a separate door, provided an ideal place for the police to monitor activity into and out of the room.

Lynn regretted not being there earlier the morning of the murder attempt, assuming that the whole thing never could have occurred had she been present. Jack had assured her that her place had been at home with the children, taking care of the family as she normally did.

Besides, he spent most of his time sleeping. He needed rest ... although not the eternal rest that he had almost achieved!

That thought continued with him throughout his waking moments.

* * * *

Captain Leonard arrived across from the office complex a few minutes early. He surveyed the front of the building from his car before exiting it and then walked across the street to the designated meeting area.

An unmarked squad car sat a short distance behind the captain's vehicle. The two occupants, plainclothes detectives, were prepared to spring to his rescue on his command, or at the first sign of anything they deemed unusual or threatening.

The captain wore a "wire", a microphone taped to his body, so that the entire conversation with the unknown caller could be both monitored by the backup personnel and recorded.

"I'm in position" he indicated to his backup crew.

"Captain, someone is approaching from your right."

Glancing in that direction, a figure appeared in front of the building, moving directly in his path.

"Well, good evening, Doc.

Working late tonight?"

While he recognized many of the Midsouth physicians on sight, he didn't always remember their names.

The figure hesitated for a moment, and then turned toward him.

"Don't you know why I'm here?"

Captain Leonard suddenly recognized the voice.

"*You're the one who called?*"

"Yes. Can we go up to my office to discuss this? I want to tell you what I know before I change my mind. I've got to get this off my chest. It's all just gone too far."

"Of course." He nodded in agreement and followed the weary figure to the elevator in the entrance foyer. He felt safe now that he recognized the mystery caller, although he couldn't comprehend how this individual ... previously mentioned by Jack Davidson as one of the people being investigated by him at Midsouth ... could be involved in such a complex affair.

He cautiously nodded toward his crew that everything was all right and proceeded to follow the figure into the building.

In the security of his office, the once proud physician laid out the facts as he knew them, sparing no detail. And when he had finished, he felt better ... even though the captain could not promise any deals.

Captain Leonard did, however, promise to make a plea for clemency since the information obtained would certainly help put a swift end to the whole dastardly affair.

Plans were immediately made for an early morning roundup of those involved.

Chapter 32

▼

Evansville, N.C.—December 5, 2005

The members of the *project* group had never assembled together in one place. Decisions had always come from the top; given the method of entry of most of its members, there was no call for discussion by the first line players.

They gathered at Russ Callahan's home to discuss their next move. Jack Davidson was still very much alive despite several attempts to silence him. Tempers flared as members realized that their careers and their very lives were about to crumble if the matter could not be settled in a manner that continued to protect their anonymity.

After a brief heated discussion, with a few dissenters appalled by the news of what had taken place without their knowledge, the group still felt that the best solution was to let their hired gang finish the job. For any of them to try something ... and be apprehended ... would immediately place the entire group in the spotlight.

Dave Fortner was conspicuously absent.

Bill remained neutral during the discussion, not wanting to appear too anxious and possibly tip his hand concerning the exit strategy he had devised. His mind was on South America.

He had contacted an old acquaintance from medical school that now worked in Brazil and who had agreed to help him hide out while he worked on creating a new identity. Perhaps it wasn't the greatest plan, but it was the best he could do on short notice.

He would worry about the details of his post-Evansville life after his arrival there. With one more day to endure, he wasn't sure if his stomach could handle the torture. Hopefully, extricating himself from the site of the problem would help soothe his pain.

At the hospital, members of Captain Leonard's team assigned to Jack Davidson were positioned in and around his new fourth floor room, posing as nurses, orderlies or lab techs. Medical personnel directly involved with his care had been apprised of their presence, and admonished to keep careful watch for anyone or anything unusual in the vicinity of the room.

Disguised detectives went about performing menial tasks to legitimize their presence and dispel boredom. Keeping alert and focused becomes the hardest part of the assignment ... as they waited for a possible Trojan horse to appear.

* * * *

Midsouth—December 2, 2005

Amidst all the other stomach-churning activities that had beset Bill's routine recently had been a request several weeks earlier for *project* patient records by Dr. Susan Aldrich from the state medical board. Then a meeting of the two scheduled for the day after Jack's accident had been necessarily postponed ... but now she insisted on meeting with Bill on the seventh ... a meeting that he planned never to take place.

* * * *

Midsouth—December 6, 2005

Russ Callahan was an infrequent visitor to the patient floors at Midsouth. As a radiologist, business usually came to him at his ground floor department offices and diagnostic suites. Occasionally, members of his department made bedside visits to evaluate patients before special procedures.

His presence on the fourth floor orthopedic ward that morning was, therefore, uncommon but not alarming to the nursing staff, most of whom recognized him on sight. As he exited the elevator and made the turn toward Jack's new room, he stopped to talk with several colleagues before entering.

Jack's nurse was just finishing his morning bath and excused herself.

"Well, Russ, my old friend. What brings you way up here? Things must be slow in x-ray."

"Jack. You look great!

I'm sorry that I haven't been to see you before this ... but I figured there would be lots of visitors while you were in the I.C.U. Darwin and Ben have been keeping me up to date on your condition.

Actually, the department is very busy, but I thought I'd take a few minutes to stop by and say hello since I was already on the floor seeing a consult."

"There has been a parade of people in and out. As physicians we don't often appreciate just how many people disturb our patients during the course of a day ... especially in the I.C.U. It's a wonder that they get any rest at all."

Jack couldn't help but notice that while he was talking, Russ seemed distracted and had been playing with an object in his white lab coat pocket, as if hiding something.

And he continued to pace the floor nervously.

"Russ, you look like you're a little anxious about something. Is anything ..."

Before Jack could finish his sentence, Russ pulled a syringe from his pocket and reached up to insert it into the IV infusion port.

"Jack, I'm sorry about this ... but you leave us no choice. If you just hadn't meddled into our affairs ..."

Russ was startled as the door to the room suddenly flew open, admitting several of the undercover police who had been stationed nearby. They quickly wrestled him to the floor, subdued him and placed handcuffs on his wrists, now behind his back. The syringe, contents intact, fell to the floor. One officer picked it up while the other read him his rights.

"Dr. Russell Callahan, you are under arrest for the attempted murder of Dr. Jack Davidson. You have the right to remain silent ..." He continued with the Miranda warning and advised him of his right to legal counsel.

The expression on Russ' face was one of sheer terror.

"How did you know?" he said, looking at Jack.

"We didn't. We suspected several members of the medical staff, but **certainly** not you. We were fairly sure someone was going to make another attempt on my life after two failures.

You and your associates, whoever they are, surely must think that I know something very important to go to all this trouble ... I mean, you've just ruined your whole career. The police have a camera in the T.V. up there."

Jack pointed to the T.V. mounted high above the bed on the wall.

"It's all on tape ... what you attempted to do to me. How could you do such a thing? I thought we were friends." Jack stared Russ right in the eye as he spoke.

"I want to speak to an attorney" was Russ's only reply. He turned away from Jack, uncomfortable with maintaining eye contact.

"Come with us, Dr. Callahan" said the officer. They made their way to the elevator amidst the incredulous stares of numerous hospital employees and visitors.

Russ, obviously humiliated by the experience, tried to hide his face from full view, but to little avail.

Reality had come full circle and smacked Russ Callahan right in the face. He stood exposed to the public: a villain caught in the act. It hurt to be on public display ... and it was only the beginning of his ordeal.

* * * *

News of Russ Callahan's arrest spread quickly throughout the medical center, putting the few members of the group not already in custody in a panic state. Armed with the information provided to Captain Leonard the night before, the Centerville Police had descended upon them *en masse* earlier that morning. Only Bill remained at large and managed to evade the police ... briefly.

At the airport, Bill Smithson awaited the departure of his Miami-bound flight, unaware of the events that had unfolded at the hospital and around town. He sat as inconspicuously as possible in a corner of the waiting area.

"Five minutes to go" he thought to himself, as he popped several Tums into his mouth.

At last, the announcement he had longed for.

"Ladies and gentlemen. This is the initial boarding call for USAir flight 383 to Miami. First class passengers may board anytime. At this time only passengers needing assistance ... may board."

He had heard the litany a thousand times.

"Just get to me! Call row thirty-two!" he thought to himself.

Finally, the call came. As he walked toward the door of the jetway, he noticed two official looking gentlemen approaching the ticket agent. Stalling the line momentarily, they then moved off to the side.

The ticket agent resumed her job.

Bill's paranoia had assumed complete control now. His anxiety reached new heights. His heart raced.

"Who are they and what could they possibly want?"

Suddenly, they turned and began walking directly toward him, causing him to break immediately into a full run towards the closest exit to the basement level.

But he was no match for the younger agents. They caught him before he reached the baggage claim carousels.

"Bill Smithson, I am Special Agent Carlson and this is Agent Carletti, State Bureau of Investigation. You are under arrest for suspicion of fraud and conspiracy to commit murder."

They flashed their badges as they advised him of his rights and applied handcuffs. Then they led him through the terminal to a waiting van.

Matters for Bill were made even worse by the presence of a local T.V. crew setting up to shoot a documentary on the history and progress of aviation in York County. Seizing upon the serendipitous opportunity to catch news in the making, the crew instantly began to film the whole affair.

At the police station, Bill found himself in the company of the other members of his group. Even he was astounded when he heard the news of Russ's attempt to kill Jack Davidson, since the consensus the day before was to let the hired gang finish the job.

But Russ had unilaterally decided that something needed to be done fast ... and right, and so he had undertaken the task of ridding the group of their major liability. He just hadn't been clever enough to suspect a surveillance camera in the room.

Newsbreaks on radio and T.V., and special editions of newspapers immediately began announcing the biggest story to hit Evansville in years. Later that day, a complete and accurate list of the incarcerated, along with a substantially correct story, was published; but it would be some time before the full facts would be known and reported to the public.

The six o'clock report on Centerville's Channel Eight led off with the following exclusive story:

"Early this morning, a joint task force comprised of members of the Centerville Police Department, the State Bureau of Investigation, and the F.B.I. arrested a substantial number of physicians and medical personnel associated with Midsouth Regional Medical Center. This afternoon, the last known member of this group, Bill Smithson, M.D., President and CEO of Midsouth, was apprehended at Evansville Regional Airport, where he was preparing to board a flight to Miami with connections to Sao Paulo, Brazil.

The group allegedly was involved in defrauding the federal and state governments, as well as insurance companies, by performing unnecessary medical, radiological and surgical procedures. It is expected that assault and other charges will be forthcoming from the innocently involved patients.

On an even more serious note, the group has been charged collectively as accomplices in the attempted murder of prominent local surgeon, Dr. Jack Davidson ... and with arson in the fire that consumed his office approximately one month earlier.

The State Medical Board is also pursuing the investigation of the death of a patient who had undergone a radiologic procedure by several of the arrested physicians to determine if additional murder charges might be filed.

It is presumed that Dr. Davidson, who had been conducting a revue study for Midsouth, inadvertently stumbled onto the group's activities. Dr. Davidson serves as Chief of Surgery at that institution.

Dr. Russ Callahan, Chairman of Radiology at Midsouth, was arrested and separately charged with the attempted murder of Dr. Davidson. He was caught on surveillance videotape attempting to inject currently unknown substances into Dr. Davidson's IV line.

That film will be broadcast by this station if and when it is released by the Evansville Police.

One member of the group, currently unidentified, served as an informant to the police several days earlier.

The following is a list of those in custody:

- Russell Callahan, M.D., Chairman of Radiology at Midsouth
- William Smithson, M.D., President and CEO, Midsouth
- David Fortner, M.D., General Surgeon and member of the medical staff at Midsouth
- Sarah Coleman Fortner, R.N., wife of Dr. Fortner and former Vice President of Patient Care at Midsouth
- Michael Herman, M.D., member of the Department of Pathology at Midsouth and Director of Hematology/Blood Bank
- Frank Li, M.D., Chairman of Emergency Medicine at Midsouth
- Kevin Bledsoe, M.D., gastroenterologist and member of the medical staff at Midsouth
- Carl Hauser, M.D., family physician and member of the medical staff at Midsouth

- Danielle Morgan Herman, wife of Dr. Herman and x-ray technology supervisor at Midsouth
- Linda Young, x-ray technologist at Midsouth

Dr. Jack Davidson, the target of the several murder attempts by hired gang members, as well as by Dr. Callahan, had been recovering from an almost fatal motor vehicle accident when today's attempt on his life occurred. He sustained no additional injuries. It is believed that the vehicle incident was actually a first attempt on his life.

Further details will be made known by this station when they become available."

Chapter 33

Evansville, N.C.—December 7, 2005

Evansville was buzzing!

The media had unleashed a blitz of stories concerning the arrests, presenting the facts as they were known. They were widely disseminated by every newspaper, radio and television station locally as well as statewide. Due to the numbers of people involved, and the fact that the story involved *doctors* and *medical matters*, the national press and the tabloids were quick to exploit it as well.

Speculation lies just one step ahead of facts in the journalistic world. Any story involving doctors, nurses and hospital personnel would have to assume that greed and power and sex would be involved, the very essence of *tabloid journalism*.

The real facts, however, would only emerge over the ensuing several weeks as the individual members of the group were interrogated and allowed to tell their stories.

Although he had been advised to the contrary by his personal attorney, Dave Fortner felt obligated to tell all that he knew to the assembled group of detectives, counsel and stenographers in order to clear his conscience.

* * * *

Evansville, N.C.—December 15, 2005

While definitely unconventional in the annals of the legal system, most of the incarcerated wanted to tell their stories to an assemblage of local police and legal counsel as soon as possible.

Together and separately, they were thoroughly embarrassed by their actions contrary to the pledges they had made to their respective medical, nursing and allied professions regarding the sacred trust of patient care.

And mostly, the majority were sorry for the actions taken against one of their own: Dr. Jack Davidson.

Interrogation Number One:
Dave Fortner, M.D.

Captain Leonard: "Dr. Fortner, would you explain to us the exact nature of your group's activity?"

Dave Fortner: "We had a group of primary care doctors who referred patients either directly to me or to Dr. Kevin Bledsoe for evaluation of possible gallbladder disease. When we started, it was only a means to get legitimate patients to me exclusively and bypass some of the other surgeons.

But as time went on, and we weren't doing enough business, we started creating our own surgical problems."

Captain Leonard: "Can you elaborate on that, Dr. Fortner? How were you able to 'create' problems?"

Dave Fortner: "We started what came to be called simply the *project*. We took patients who presented to our primary care doctors with vague abdominal pain and made them sick by injecting a concoction created by Dr. Mike Herman into their common bile duct while Dr. Bledsoe was performing ERCP. Dr. Russ Callahan was the transport man who got the vial from Dr. Herman and handed it to Dr. Bledsoe at the proper time during the procedure."

Captain Leonard: "So Drs. Callahan and Bledsoe are the brains behind the *project* along with you?"

Dave Fortner: "No, Captain. You've got it all wrong.
We're not the brains behind this.
My wife, Sarah Coleman, is."

There was a sudden gasp among the assemblage.

Captain Leonard: "Dr. Fortner, pardon me for being confused, but how can she be behind it when it involves medical evaluations and procedures.

Your wife is a nurse, not a doctor, correct?"

Dave Fortner: "Captain, it's a long and involved story, so I'll try to explain it as best I can.

It all began several years before our marriage.

I first met Sarah when she came to work as a nurse in the Intensive Care Unit at Midsouth. She had a 'significant other' at the time. But following their breakup, things began to change between us. She became aggressive in her pursuit of me.

We were kind of like teenagers at first. Just routine simple dates … like dinner and a movie. Nothing fancy and no sex." He blushed as he hesitated, but then continued.

"When she found out that I owned and flew my own plane, she asked if I would take her flying. That's when we began taking trips together down to the coast where I knew of an old remote airstrip near a small lake. After a few visits there, we became intimate with each other.

From then on, I was hooked. We began spending all of our free time together. That's when the thought of marriage first entered my mind. But the turning point came when I invited Sarah to join me on a trip to Hawaii, where I went to attend a medical conference. While we were in Honolulu, she asked if we could visit a little town called ***Hana***, on the eastern end of Maui.

Being basically shy, I though at that point in my life that I must be the luckiest guy alive to have someone as beautiful and charming as my girl.

I guess I was just plain naïve.

When we got just beyond ***Hana***, we found a secluded beach. That's when she suggested that we spend the night there together … just the two of us. Sarah promised me an unforgettable night if I agreed.

Since our flight home wasn't until late the following afternoon, we stayed … I mean, who could refuse an offer like that?

Well, the night was everything she promised … and more, if you know what I mean? I was exhausted by the time morning came. On the way back to the hotel to collect our things was the first time that she mentioned the scheme that we later referred to as the ***project.***

At that point in time, I was so enamored with her, that the thought never occurred to me that the whole thing had been planned out by her well in advance.

I knew I wanted to marry Sarah. I naturally thought that she was kidding about the whole fraud scheme, and dismissed it in my mind. She didn't bring it up again for some time, so I assumed it had just been a joke ... although not a particularly good one.

I knew nothing of her true past at that time. I only knew what she had told me, and I certainly had no reason to believe it wasn't true.

If I had known then what I know now, believe me I would never have gotten involved in this mess.

Since I'm the one who invited her to go to Hawaii, it's hard to believe that what she accomplished obviously was something that she had been planning for most of her life. She just needed the right people and the right circumstances to carry out her plan. Unfortunately, I became the main instrument of her plan, and *Hana* provided the setting for her to secure my help."

Captain Leonard: "Dr. Fortner, I ... and I'm sure the rest of the people here are confused about your wife and her plan. Can you clarify that for us?"

Dave Fortner: "Just be patient with me. I'm getting to that. After our return to Evansville from Hawaii, we got engaged and went ahead and announced our wedding plans. Then, after the wedding, came the bombshell!

She brought up her plan again. Only this time she spelled it out in fine detail. It was obvious that she had been working on it for a long time. Her immediate need was a surgeon to implement it ... *me*. She needed other physicians as well, and that's when I found out that she and her sisters had been busy 'recruiting' people.

You see, I learned that she had her sisters trained to do professional photography ... and that they had been there at *Hana*, taking pictures of Sarah and me naked ... making love on the beach.

That's when I learned of her blackmail scheme ... how she 'recruited' and kept the people she needed to carry out her crazed plan. She and her sisters threatened to use the pictures if we didn't cooperate. They threatened to release the pictures to the media if we didn't *choose* to ally with her in the *project*.

With this added 'incentive', the promise of easy money, and continued 'good times' at home with Sarah, I had no real choice ... I mean what would you have done, threatened with ruining your career ... and your life?"

Dave stopped and stared around the room at those listening to his story.

What **would** they have done?

The room was deathly quiet. Most stared away from Dave's peering eyes, glad that they didn't have to answer the question.

"I was never rich. Sarah's plan changed all that. It would've been a lot to pass up. And there was the constant threat of exposure that she threatened me with.

She indicated that she already had others willing to help ... although she didn't say how she had recruited them, and I didn't ask since I guess I didn't really want to know. At the time, I was either too much in love or too stupid to realize that there had to be more to all this than was immediately obvious.

She leaked the details to me a little bit at a time, as though she had just thought of them. In Maui, she talked of getting a few physicians together to send us gallbladder patients ... sort of a kickback scheme where I thought we would pay them for their referrals. Of course, she had already 'recruited' people who were willing to work for other reasons.

Then we started faking x-rays and pathology reports to match. Drs. Callahan and Herman provided the expertise needed in those two areas.

When she decided we could make even more money if we actually made people sick, Dr. Kevin Bledsoe was recruited. Dr. Herman concocted a mixture of bacteria and small stones that was injected into the common bile duct during an ERCP exam.

To get more patients referred into the system, Drs. Li and Hauser were brought in. Both were in desperate financial need at the time, and accepted our offer for some quick and easy money.

There was a large flow of patients from our primary care people to Kevin Bledsoe, and then to me. The people who didn't perform procedures or surgery were given an incentive bonus for each patient. That way the wealth was distributed among all our personnel and it reduced the chances of someone deciding to bail-out on the group. And if anyone dared to expose the plot, they would be equally culpable.

Not to mention, there was the constant threat of the pictures!

And then there was Bill Smithson. He had been Sarah's lover shortly after his marriage to his current wife, Maggie. Sarah knew that with him involved, she could be assured of having someone that could facilitate things around the institution."

Captain Leonard: "Dr. Fortner, why don't we take a short break. You've been talking for over an hour. We'll take a short recess in case anyone needs to use the restroom or get some coffee.

* * * *

The session resumed after a short interval.

Captain Leonard: "Dr. Fortner, let me remind you that when it comes to matters about your wife, you don't have to testify?"

Dave: "Yes. But for my sanity, and hopefully for hers, I'd like to continue.

Several times since our marriage, I decided I didn't want to continue with the deception. And that's when she threatened me with pictures of me engaged in sex with another woman.

I was stunned and embarrassed. It was my only other sexual encounter with a woman in my entire lifetime. I couldn't possibly imagine how the pictures had been taken, in the privacy of the other woman's home.

I assumed that the other woman had sent them to her after our wedding out of jealousy ... and to extort money from us.

But when I told Sarah the whole story ... it had happened before we were engaged, her response wasn't what I would have expected. She made no mention of extortion demands from the other woman, or what she intended to do about her.

Instead, she said she would expose me as an adulterer and sue me for divorce if I didn't continue with the ***project***. And of course, that meant taking most of my future earnings and our house and leaving me little else.

I was trapped no matter which way I turned.

And then she became violent at times ... something I had never seen her do before. Frankly, she scared me. I had no choice but to continue. She began spending money like it was going out of style and forced me to work harder to keep up with her growing bad habit.

My life has been nothing but pure hell since all this began."

Dave lost his composure, and was almost in tears.

"I know you must think me weak for the way I acted. But there's even more. Sarah finally informed me that the woman in the picture was married. I was afraid that her husband might find out about our affair ... and I frankly didn't know what he might do to me. I had no idea that she was a married woman ... she told me she was single.

As I said earlier, it never occurred to me that Sarah was behind the thing all along. You see, the woman I had the affair with was Sarah's sister. And it had all been a part of her twisted plot to have all the men she needed for her ***project*** set up so that they could be blackmailed if they ever threatened to walk out on her.

Not to mention, getting even with members of the medical profession ... her main motive.

Sarah has twin sisters who live and work right here in Evansville ... at Midsouth.

Their father was a doctor who was extremely mean to them as children. Sarah voluntarily accepted punishment due her two little sisters. In return, they vowed to help her avenge their father's cruelty.

But then an unfortunate thing happened.

Their father was killed in an automobile accident, leaving them no one on whom to extract that revenge ... except members of their father's profession.

The girls left their home and stepmother and became educated before coming to Evansville, where we all became victims of bad timing. Midsouth's massive recruiting campaign at the time they were seeking a place to carry out their scheme led them here.

The twins were available to do anything that she needed them to do ... including having affairs with men. They took pictures of the men engaging in sexual activities at several locations including their personal apartments and a cottage at the beach. The pictures were always taken in a way to expose the man's face and never the woman's.

You'll have to admit that it was beautifully conceived and executed by Sarah and her sisters. All this time they worked together at Midsouth, and people never even suspected their relationship."

Captain Leonard: "Dr. Fortner, could you please tell us who these two sisters are?"

Dave Fortner: "Captain Leonard, they are the other two women you have in custody: Danielle Morgan Herman, Mike Herman's wife, and Linda Young, who was Russ Callahan's lover."

The room erupted with whispers as people questioned how it had been possible for the trio to carry on such deception.

Captain Leonard: "You're saying that your wife, Sarah, and these two women are sisters ... even though they all have different names and don't look the least bit alike? And that they carried out this elaborate plot to avenge their physician father who died in an accident?

Who else knows about this?"

Dave Fortner: "That's correct. And no one but me knew about it until now ... and I only learned about it in the past few weeks.

Each of the three moved here at a slightly different time. They held jobs in close proximity to one another at Midsouth ... as well as to their victims. Each had a different last name and listed a different birthplace and claimed to be an only child. And each had had some minor plastic surgery to alter their facial features.

So now you know *Hana's Secret* ... which after today will be a secret no more."

Dave was done and appeared both relieved and depressed at the same time. Although he was glad to have the story out in the open, he knew that he would now have to face the consequences of his actions, and forever be considered a traitor to his group.

* * * *

Captain Leonard returned to his office where he promptly received an urgent call from the desk sergeant at the York County Jail informing him that Bill Smithson had been taken to the emergency room at Midsouth. He had been complaining about stomach pains since his arrest, and had suddenly become extremely ill.

Captain Leonard felt compelled to go to the hospital to determine the gravity of the problem. He found Dr. Lem Samuels, the emergency room physician attending Bill Smithson, who informed him that Bill had a perforated stomach ulcer and would require urgent surgery.

Dr. Ben Thomas arrived and arranged to perform the procedure immediately.

"Captain Leonard, he'll need to have this ulcer problem fixed urgently, and then will probably need to be in the hospital for about a week. I'll call you when I'm finished and let you know how things went. He should be o.k. although he'll need to be in the I.C.U. for a few days."

"Thanks for your help, Dr. Thomas. We'll arrange for a guard to be posted outside his room while he is here."

* * * *

Evansville, N.C.—December 16, 2005

When testimony continued the following day, each of the other men involved had little to say or refused to testify on advice of counsel. Each felt victimized by the way they had been coerced into participating in the Coleman/Fortner scheme.

Russ Callahan added little to his particularly difficult situation. Faced with loss of profession and family if Jack Davidson were allowed to proceed with his investigation, he had felt it necessary to eliminate him by the quickest means possible. However, he obviously didn't think the whole thing through, and should have suspected that the police would be watching everyone ... especially medical people ... coming into Jack's room.

Linda Young was now a faded memory. He would have to decide if the occasional moments of stolen bliss with her had all been worthwhile.

Frank Li was a pathetic case as well. He and Jack had been good friends, as had their wives. He had lost money in several bad real estate deals and had been desperate for cash. He had confided his situation to Bill Smithson, who in turn mentioned it to Sarah. She brought him in with the promise of quick money. His immediate problem had been solved, but the long-term ramifications would ultimately destroy his marriage, his career and his friendship with Jack Davidson.

Bill Smithson stood to lose as much or more than anyone. Sarah had convinced him to hire the gang to kill Jack Davidson when the office fire had failed to deter his efforts to investigate Dave Fortner and the *"project."*

Due to his being in the hospital recovering from surgery, he was not available to testify.

Mike Herman was a particularly unfortunate case. He had been raised in a caring family that had inculcated high morals in its children. Despite being drawn into a sexual affair with Danielle Morgan, he was prepared to rectify the situation by marrying her when she announced that she was pregnant with his child. However, he didn't suspect that he was being victimized ... that she was not pregnant at the time and that the group was in desperate need of a pathologist.

Danielle had taken him to her home "studio" and later to the beach cottage to be photographed like the others. The films, eventually found and reviewed by the police, were professionally done and edited, exposing the men full face while always being careful to protect the identities of the women.

"Do you know how it makes a man feel ... first to think you're in love with someone who you believe is going to have your baby ... and then to find out that not only have you been used, but that your very life and career are being taken from you at the same time?

I was responsible for concocting the mixture of bacteria and sludge that Kevin Bledsoe injected during his ERCP procedures, and I changed some of the reports and samples ... but I had nothing to do with the decisions concerning injuring or eliminating Jack Davidson."

Each man except Russ Callahan tried to make that point perfectly clear.

"And the one death that occurred during an ERCP, that caused a lot of attention and prompted many investigations, turned out to be an explainable drug reaction.

Isn't it strange how life often turns on a dime?"

The women would begin their testimonies later.

* * * *

Evansville, N.C.—December 20, 2005
Interrogation Number Two:
Sarah Coleman Fortner

She had remained in an almost trance-like state since her arrest and incarceration in the York County Jail. After so many years of planning, and meticulous execution of the plan with the help of her obedient sisters, it had met with only limited success.

After all, she had succeeded in ruining the lives of a number of doctors ... but it had all come to a screeching halt thanks to the meddling of the do-gooder Dr. Jack Davidson ... and the betrayal by her own husband, whom she thought she had trained better. At the outset of the session, her seething anger was immediately obvious.

Captain Leonard: "Mrs. Fortner, I'm sure this is a trying time for you. If you will, please tell us about this scheme you and your sisters carried out at Midsouth."

Sarah: "Please, just call me Sarah. I don't want to be known by that traitor's last name.

Yes, it was *I* who planned the whole thing," she said in a haughty tone, as if she were proud of her misdeeds ... as indeed she was.

"My sisters only helped. I taught them to carry out my orders ... and they did that very well. I took care of them when they were little, and this was their way of repaying me.

Daddies are supposed to take care of their little girls ... and love them ... and spoil them.

But not our daddy.

He was an all important **doctor**."

The disdain for him and the whole profession he represented in her mind was obvious from her facial expression and her intonation. She had an accentuated smirk on her face at the enunciation of the word **doctor.**

"He was always too busy to take us places or do things with us. And when he was home, he was a tyrant. He was constantly critical of the things we did. Though we tried very hard, we were never able to please him. He thought everyone should be as smart as he was. He expected too much from us. We were just little girls, and when we couldn't do what he demanded, he punished us severely."

Squirming in her chair as she recounted these obviously uncomfortable times from her childhood, she appeared to be reliving them as she spoke.

"He made us study and work and practice all the time. While our friends were allowed to play, we were constantly reminded that 'idleness is the devil's workshop'. And if we didn't do things to his satisfaction … and we never did—he would punish us.

He would spank us with an old razor strap he got from a barbershop. And then he would lock us up in **that** dark room for hours at a time so that we could think about our transgressions … that's what he called them … **transgressions**.

We were too young for that kind of treatment, especially my little sisters. When I volunteered to take their punishment for them, I think he thought that noble of me … but he never lessened the severity of the punishment, or the time in **that** dark room."

She curled up in the chair, pulling her legs up against her torso with her arms, at the mention of this obviously foreboding place that she had locked in her memory.

"I was always so scared. When he finally let me out, I would get together with my sisters and talk about the day when we would get even with him and our mother.

She wasn't our real mother. Daddy was remarried. She never tried to help us or get him to stop punishing us. She was too busy enjoying her role as the doctor's wife and wouldn't do anything to jeopardize that.

She hated us."

Sarah began to cry. The assemblage said nothing, feeling empathy for her situation, and trying to imagine how alone and abandoned she and her sisters must have felt.

Suddenly, she shot up in the chair. There was an aura of confidence about her as she resumed speaking. Her face was radiant, and the tears had disappeared.

It was like a reincarnation!

"We had to get even. We decided that when we got older, we would run away from home. We wanted them to experience the pain of loneliness and separation ... and guilt."

Apparent sadness overcame her again. The sparkle disappeared from her eyes replaced by melancholy.

"But then he died ... **died!**

Our daddy was killed in an automobile accident one night on the way home from a party at the hospital. I was still locked in **that** room when the police came to tell us what happened. Mother was hurt and at the hospital ... but she survived. She never helped us after that even though she was all we had. After all, we weren't hers. We never got the chance to get even with him ... and she had it coming too ... for not coming to our rescue. But we got even finally."

The look of confidence returned in her eyes.

"As soon as my sisters finished high school, we moved out on our own. I finished nursing school while my sisters became x-ray techs. During that time I conceived the plan. I figured if I couldn't get even with my father, I could at least get even with others in his profession who must be as evil as he was.

It took quite a while to refine my plan until I knew that it could work. All we had to do was find the right place to carry it out. A little luck brought us to Evansville and all this!"

Her eyes beamed as she indubitably thought of those brought down by her plan. Her fate seemed of little, if any, concern. After all, she had succeeded in raining down misery on a substantial number of people in the medical profession.

"Evansville was purely a random choice. When we saw ads that Midsouth was recruiting people in nursing and radiology, it was the perfect choice since it was far enough away from home for no one to know us, and large enough to maintain anonymity as we went about setting up the *project*.

My first recruit was Bill Smithson." An unusually pleasing glow overtook her face as she described the circumstances under which she was able to seduce him.

"He had remarried after his first wife died. Maggie was working hard at the hospital, trying to be the good wife, but leaving him lonely. So he just fell right into my arms. Considering the important position he occupied at Midsouth, I knew that once he was in my grasp we could pull the whole thing off.

My sisters, meanwhile, were busy with discreet affairs of their own with numerous doctors on the medical staff, assuring us a group of 'players' when we needed them.

When I met my husband, I knew it could be done. When he invited me to go to Hawaii with him, I knew I could get the insurance we might eventually need. My sisters did the rest of the work.

Hana was the key.

I showed him the time of his life as promised and I knew after Hana that he would do anything I asked of him.

There are advantages to being female, you know!"

She twisted toward the men in the audience as she enunciated the word "female". Her dress, which had been at knee level, now rose to the top of her thighs, causing the men present to lose control of the urge to ogle her.

"After that night in ***Hana***, I knew I had him ... I knew that I could get him to do anything I asked. I slowly brought him into my personal world, never trusting him with the entire truth about my sisters and me until just recently.

We discussed the ***project*** again after our engagement, but he was still reluctant. I waited until after we were married to convince him that there were other ways to bring him around if necessary."

The meaning of "other ways" was now quite clear.

"I made sure my sisters mastered photography while they were in x-ray tech school, should it be necessary to coerce people into joining us ... or staying with us. We made sure that we had movies of all our subjects taken at our favorite locations."

The ferocity in her voice and the gleam in her eye indicated just how proud she was of the attention to detail she had given every facet of the scheme.

"Those poor stupid ***doctors*** never knew what was about to hit them!

We were able to recruit all the people we needed once Bill Smithson was in the fold. Drs. Li and Hauser, desperate for money, delivered us the people we needed to get things really going."

Her temperament returned to anger as her tonal quality coarsened once again.

"And then that damn Dr. Jack Davidson had to come along and spoil everything. He was always sticking his nose where it wasn't supposed to be. You'd think that he could have taken a friendly hint when we burned down his office and killed his dog.

But still he kept at it.

And then he couldn't even die in that damn wreck we arranged!"

The rage abated as she assumed the supplicant role.

"Christ! Where do people like him come from anyway? Why couldn't he have been ***our daddy?*** Then we wouldn't have had to hate doctors so."

She withdrew into the corner of her chair and turned to one side with her knees flexed. An occasional whimper soon gave way to a flood of tears accompanied by constant sobbing.

Observers in the room, moved by this profound display of pathos, were on the verge of joining her. Despite the evil she had wrought, it was difficult not to feel empathy for Sarah.

So revenge had been the motive ... not greed or lust or power as had been assumed.

The interview appeared to be at an end when the slight figure of a woman recoiled from her slouched position in the chair and began to speak ... first in a barely audible whisper but rapidly proceeding to a violent loud cry.

"Daddy! Please let me out of this room. Oh please. I'll be good, I promise. Don't hit me any more ... and leave Janie and Marie alone. They're so afraid of you. They never did anything to hurt you or mother.

Why do you hate us all so?

No! No!"

Recoiling into the chair, she now held up her arms like someone fending off an attack, and then began to sob once more.

She lay momentarily paralyzed.

Captain Leonard consulted the precinct psychiatrist who had been observing her behavior, asking that he recommend an appropriate course of action.

And who were Janie and Marie? Things were becoming more confused.

Dr. Foxworth observed her for a few minutes.

"Let's watch and see what she does, as long as she doesn't become violent to anyone present. She may be about to reveal something important."

After three or four additional minutes in this trance, she turned and began to talk as if she were conversing with her husband.

"Oh Dave, you will love me and take care of me, won't you? I've worked long enough ... now I just want to be here for you. I'll be sexy for you ... I'll do whatever you want if you'll just do this one thing for me."

There was a singular self-confidence in her voice as she spoke.

Then instantly, her persona changed again ... the confidence gone ... suddenly, like light when the power fails.

Still another instant and a wicked smile spread across her face.

"Dave. I have a surprise for you.

You *will* be the leader of the *project* Dave.

Do you remember that night in **Hana** Dave? It wasn't the most incredible night of your life for nothing. Everything has a price, Dave ... and now it's your turn to pay the piper."

Her tone continued firm and steady.

"These are for you, my darling husband. What do you think that this has all been about ... love? I don't need your love, Dave. I only need you to carry out my plan. I think you need to look at these before you say no."

She gestured as if handing something to someone.

"How do you like the pictures, Dave? I bet you never saw yourself naked on a beach before, making love to a woman.

How did I get the pictures?" She seemed to be answering an unspoken question.

"That night on the beach at **Hana** ... you remember the noises on the other side of the dunes? Well, I told you it was nothing of concern for you.

But I lied!" She boldly enunciated the words.

"It was my sisters doing what I asked of them ... getting a little added insurance in case you said no to my plan.

You're the key to it all Dave. I had to make sure you played the game ... one way or another."

She smiled. "I'm so glad you agreed, Dave."

"And you, Maggie ... well, you got what was coming to you, too."

She slid down into her chair and appeared to fall asleep.

Captain Leonard turned to Dr. Foxworth.

"What is your professional opinion of her performance?"

"I think she could honestly represent a case of true multiple personalities. She needs to go to the state mental facility in Raleigh for observation and probable long-term psychiatric care. With your permission, I'll make the arrangements."

"Thank you."

Captain Leonard asked the F.B.I. for help in establishing the true identities of Janie and Marie ... and Maggie.

Evansville, N.C.—December 27, 2005
Interrogation Number Three:
Jack Davidson, M.D.

Jim Akins had placed the rod in Jack's broken femur the day after the arrests so that he could then begin his final convalescent phase. He was able to leave the hospital a few days later and continue his physical therapy as an outpatient. As promised, Jack arranged to meet Captain Leonard and his staff the day after discharge from Midsouth. He was brought into the room in a wheelchair.

"Dr. Davidson, thanks for coming in today. On behalf of my entire staff, Merry Christmas to you and your family.

Before you tell us your story, let me tell you what our laboratory learned about the contents of the syringe that Dr. Callahan brought to your room.

It contained succinylcholine hydrochloride ... which as you know is a muscle-paralyzing drug ... the same drug we found in the syringe that the bogus lab person tried to inject into your IV in the I.C.U.

But, he had a second syringe in his coat pocket that contained potassium chloride ... and you know that it is rapidly fatal when given IV. It's the same combination of drugs used in legal executions.

So ... there's no question that Dr. Callahan really meant business this time. And the really clever thing was that he also carried a microcomputer that generates heart rhythms. He has confessed that he planned to hook it to your EKG monitor, so that after he injected the drugs into you, it would have continued to generate a normal heart rhythm pattern at the nurses' monitoring station.

After the drugs did their work, he would change the rhythm to ventricular fibrillation. Then he could run to the nurses' station and report something was suddenly wrong with you ... something that they could clearly see on their monitor. He would appear innocent.

The nurses would call a ***Code Blue*** ... he would be there to help with the resuscitation effort ... but you would not be able to be saved.

And Dr. Callahan would look like an almost hero."

Jack suddenly looked a little pale, more so than the anemic state he had been left in after his trauma ordeal would warrant. He imagined himself lying there paralyzed after the first injection, watching Russ inject the fatal second medication. He began sweating ... but then relaxed as he looked around the room and found himself in protected surroundings.

Captain Leonard: "Dr. Davidson, please tell us how you got involved in this mess?"

"Captain Leonard, as you know, I started the investigation of Dave Fortner at the insistence of several of my colleagues who detected some possible irregularities in his work. I seriously doubted at the outset that I would find anything of substance. But during my review of his charts several suspicious things came to my attention.

Then I was made aware that Dr. Susan Aldrich from the State Medical Board had contacted the hospital for additional information about some cases that Dr. Fortner had done that had prompted patient complaints to that authority. And then there followed the death that occurred in radiology, involving Drs. Bledsoe and Callahan. We knew that Dr. Fortner had been consulted on that patient.

After Dr. Herman's conclusions from the autopsy that the death of that patient was from a rare idiosyncratic reaction called angioedema, I was ready to conclude my investigation again. We had Dr. Herman's conclusions reviewed by an independent pathologist who concurred with his findings.

The State Medical Board was satisfied with the report and my initial recommendations.

But then came the personal attacks on me: the fire that destroyed my office that was clearly arson, and the death of my dog. As you and I concluded, it appeared that the only common denominator was something related to what I was doing at the hospital.

Working late at the hospital one evening, I had the opportunity to review some additional charts. I noticed that the same physicians were involved in virtually every case eventually operated on by Dave Fortner. Since there are multiple physicians in the radiology, pathology and emergency departments, it seemed just too much of a coincidence for the same group of names to keep coming up together randomly.

Of course, I had no way of knowing about the association of Sarah Coleman, or her sisters or Bill Smithson at that point in time. That all came as a total surprise.

It's a darn good thing that I decided to confide in you what I knew that particular day. My wife convinced me that it would be the smart play. I can be kind of hard-headed at times."

Captain Leonard shook his head in complete agreement.

"And then I still stupidly played into their hands the morning of the accident. I still didn't think that what I was investigating was so important that I would be risking my life over it.

When I realized that someone might be following me, I should have gone directly to the nearest police station, instead of playing into their hands. That's what watching too many cop shows on TV will do for you!

I thank the EMS and my colleagues who cared for me for saving my life, and you and your associates, Captain, for saving me several times at the hospital.

By the way, how did you find out about the others?"

"Your colleague, Dave Fortner, came to me right after your accident ... after he found out the truth from his wife ... that she had engineered the whole thing and was responsible for the contract on your life. We wanted to make sure that everyone involved was on our list, so we kept you under surveillance for a while in the hospital. But after two more attempts on your life, we felt it time to arrest all that we knew about, and hope we had everyone.

And fortunately, things worked out. It appears that we do have everyone associated with the Fortner affair ... and you're still with us."

Captain Leonard stood up and walked over to Jack. He extended his hand to him.

"I'd like to shake your hand and thank you for your help in bringing this whole shameful affair to an end. You risked your life several times, and we appreciate it.

And just what are your plans for the future, Dr. Davidson? Will you be able to return to work soon?"

"I've got a lot of physical therapy ahead of me. And I want to take some time off. After an attempt ... several attempts ... on your life, it's a good time for reflecting on life's priorities ... especially concerning family and career.

I'll eventually get back to practicing. With the loss of Dr. Fortner to the community, I suppose I can be busier than ever if I choose.

And I promised Midsouth that I would help them clean up the whole mess I started: there are hundreds of charts to be reviewed and analyzed. I'm sure that there will be many lawsuits stemming from this, and that I'll be getting a lot of subpoenas."

"Matthew Gates has already filed two law suits, representing the first two ladies who filed complaints with the State Medical Board: Carol Smith and Tina Rouse. Do you know either of them, Dr. Davidson?"

Jack shook his head no.

"But I'm sure their names and many others will become household names before this is all over."

"Undoubtedly" concluded the Captain.

The session ended with the entire group giving Jack a round of applause and lining up to shake his hand.

*　　*　　*　　*

After the room had been emptied, the special visitor was brought in as arranged in advance with Jack.

He was escorted into the room in handcuffs and leg irons. His request to meet with Jack was highly irregular; but thanks to his help, the affair had been concluded. So Captain Leonard had permitted it ... but only with Jack's concurrence.

"Jack", Dave Fortner began, "I'm so sorry about the way things worked out for all of us. I know that you were just doing your job as Chief of Surgery. But I want you to know that my wife has blackmailed me since we've been married, and I had been just too much of a coward to do anything about it ... until they tried to hurt you. As bad as what we were doing was, it doesn't justify murder. I couldn't believe that she would ever resort to that ... just because you were getting close to the truth.

I want you to know that even though we were never the best of friends, I always admired your abilities as a surgeon. And I have always been more than just a little jealous of the special relationship you have with the nurses, especially in the I.C.U.

So I want you to know how sorry I am that this has all happened to you, and I hope that you will accept my apology. While I'll have to share in the guilt, I wanted you to know that I had nothing to do with trying to harm you.

And I'm glad that you will be able to return to practice."

Jack sat silent for a few moments.

"Dave, it takes a big man to admit when he is wrong, especially face to face.

You must understand that I don't agree with anything you and the others did to our patients, or to me personally, regardless of motives or circumstances. You betrayed the trust of the profession by your actions.

But I do believe that you are sincere about not wanting to harm me. And for that, I accept your apology and forgive you. I only hope that the legal system can show you some leniency for your part in putting an end to this whole affair."

Jack took Dave's hand and embraced it ... and then turned away as Dave was led out of the room and returned to the York County Jail.

*   *   *   *

Jack had asked for a meeting with Frank Li, but Frank had declined. Having been a close personal friend, he was too ashamed to face Jack. Cindy had already called Lynn and offered an apology for Frank's actions. She was planning to move back home to New Hampshire, since she and her husband would probably never be able to have a normal life again. She had even hinted that she might seek a divorce after the legal action was concluded.

CHAPTER 34

▼

Evansville—December 28, 2005

<u>Interrogation Number Four:</u>
Danielle Morgan Herman
Linda Young

The final police interviews were with Sarah's two sisters, Danielle Herman and Linda Young. They corroborated the testimony given earlier by Sarah concerning the mistreatment by their father, but they elaborated a bit more.

Sarah had often been given enemas to rid her of "evil spirits", before placing her in a dark closet chained to the wall. Their father often left her there for days, forcing her to stand in her own waste, and allowing her feet and ankles to swell to the point that she was unable to wear shoes for days afterward.

At the completion of their story, Captain Leonard asked them to help clear up some obscure facts.

Captain Leonard: "Just who are the Janie and Marie that your sister Sarah referred to at the end of her testimony?"

They looked at each other momentarily.

Danielle: "I'm Janie and she's Marie," she said, pointing to Linda.

Captain Leonard: "I'm afraid I don't understand."

Danielle: "We are the Moore sisters. Sarah, whose real name is Katie, is the oldest, and we are twins. Our father was Dr. Alfred Moore, a family practitioner. We thought it best to change our names when we left Altamont ... that's our real home town."

Captain Leonard: "And what about someone named Maggie ... do you have any idea who that would be?"

The girls looked in each other's direction and momentarily laughed when they heard the question.

Linda: "You don't know, do you?

Maggie Smithson is our stepmother. It wasn't part of our original plan to get even with her apart from abandoning her just as she had abandoned us in our time of need. But by some strange twist of fate, she married Bill Smithson after we had located to Evansville. She had relocated to Chapel Hill after we left home and met Bill there while he was in medical school.

So we were able to get even with her by destroying him. And she didn't even realize it until now."

Captain Leonard: "But how could she not know ... I mean all of you work there at the medical center? Surely you must have seen each other and recognized one another."

Linda: "As part of the plan, we all had some plastic surgery done to alter our features, and we changed our hair color. Each of us wears colored contact lenses."

She reached up and took out the lens in her right eye.

Linda: "See. My eyes are brown, not blue. So it fooled you, too."

* * * *

Fingerprints later corroborated the story told by the twin sisters, Janie and Marie Moore. In addition, the Altamont Dispatch yielded stories and pictures of the tragic death of their father, Dr. Alfred Moore, in an automobile accident some fourteen years earlier. The article listed the names of the surviving family members as: Maggie Moore and three children, Katie, Janie and Marie.

Indeed, they had fooled the Evansville police just as they had the community and the medical center ... and Maggie Smithson!

Chapter 35

▼

Evansville Gazette Exclusive

by Susan Marlowe

In a story unfolding here in Evansville for the past several weeks, it has now been conclusively determined that the instigator of the plot involving unnecessary surgery, fraudulent insurance claims, and attempted murder of prominent local surgeon, Dr. Jack Davidson, has been positively identified as Katherine Sarah Moore, aka Sarah Coleman Fortner. It was revealed that the true identity of Ms. Moore and her sisters was previously unknown to anyone in Evansville except Ms. Moore's husband, Dr. David A. Fortner.

Ms. Moore (Mrs. Fortner) was formerly employed by Midsouth Regional Medical Center. She began her professional career as a registered nurse employed in the Intensive Care Unit. At the time of her retirement, she was serving as Vice President of Patient Care.

Dr. Fortner, as noted in previous editions, had been presumed to be the leader of the group.

It has also been firmly ascertained that Ms. Moore (Mrs. Fortner) has two sisters also formerly employed by Midsouth: Danielle Morgan Herman, now identified as Jane (Janie) Alma Moore; and Linda Young, now identified as Marie Michelle Moore.

Ms. Janie Moore (Danielle Herman) is the wife of Michael Herman, M.D., former Director of the Hematology Lab/Blood Bank at Midsouth. He was also implicated in the plot and is currently being held at the York County Jail.

In a story replete with intrigue, it was learned that the three sisters had been raised in Altamont, in western North Carolina. Alleged mistreatment at the hands of their abusive physician father led to their pathologic desire for revenge. Following the father's death in an automobile accident, the three continued to plan and carry out revenge against the profession he represented.

Aided by her two younger twin sisters, Sarah (Katie Moore) was able to mastermind this vicarious revenge plot that eventually involved a host of physicians and healthcare professionals at Midsouth. This included Bill Smithson, M.D., former CEO of Midsouth who had been involved in a tryst with her; Dr. Herman, husband of Danielle (Janie), and Dr. Russell Callahan, former Chief of Radiology at Midsouth, involved in an extramarital affair with Linda Young (Marie). Dr. Callahan, a member of the criminal group, also attempted the murder of Dr. Jack Davidson.

Dr. Davidson had unwittingly uncovered evidence of the group's illegal activities while investigating possible wrongdoing by Dr. Fortner. He had been appointed to that task as part of his legitimate duties as Chief of Surgery at Midsouth.

Dr. Davidson's office had previously been destroyed by fire in an attempt to discourage him from continuing the investigation. A subsequent staged accident arranged by the group nearly claimed his life.

The male members of the group, with the exceptions of Dr. Frank Li, former Chief of Emergency Medicine at Midsouth and Dr. Carl Hauser, former family practitioner in Evansville, had all been enticed into working for the group through illicit sexual encounters with the three women.

Drs. Li and Hauser, each in financial difficulty, had been victimized after agreeing to supply patients to the group in return for money.

The recruited members of the group continued to participate in its illegal activities when threatened with personal embarrassment and financial ruin. With the attempt on Dr. Jack Davidson's life, Dr. Fortner chose to come forward with a complete disclosure of the facts and a list of the group's participants.

Bill Smithson, M.D., was apprehended at Evansville Regional Airport, attempting to flee to South America. Shortly after his arrest and incarceration at York County Jail, he developed an acute illness requiring his transfer to Midsouth where he underwent emergency surgery. He is currently recuperating at that facility's I.C.U. and is expected to make a complete recovery.

Indictments of all members of the group are expected within the week. Meanwhile, numerous lawsuits have been filed by both local and out-of-town attorneys on behalf of patients involved in the unnecessary surgery and fraud scheme.

The F.B.I., Medicare and state Medicaid administration officials are looking into the extent of the group's illegal activities. A multitude of additional charges are anticipated.

All the physicians taken into custody have had summary suspensions of their medical licenses by the State Board of Medicine, pending further investigation and results of legal action.

William Smithson, M.D., has been relieved of his duties as CEO/administrator of Midsouth pending further investigation and results of legal action. Martin Ashcroft, Senior Associate Administrator at Midsouth, has been appointed acting CEO.

Katie Moore (Mrs. Fortner) has been transferred to the State Mental Facility in Raleigh for psychiatric evaluation. Her sisters are being evaluated locally for possible transfer to that facility as well.

* * * *

Evansville Gazette Exclusive

by Susan Marlowe

In a follow up to a recently published story by this author, disposition of members of the Midsouth group arrested for Medical fraud and attempted murder are as follows:

- Dr. Russell Callahan—indicted for involvement in fraudulent medical activity **and** for the attempted murder of Dr. Jack Davidson. Bond was refused.
- Dr. Frank Li—released on $500,000 bond, pending trial for fraudulent medical activity and conspiracy to commit murder.
- Dr. Carl Hauser—released on $500,000 bond, pending trial for fraudulent medical activity and conspiracy to commit murder.
- Dr. David A. Fortner—released on $1,000,000 bond, pending trial for fraudulent medical activity and conspiracy to commit murder.
- Dr. Michael Herman—released on $1,000,000 bond, pending trial for fraudulent medical activity and conspiracy to commit murder.

- Dr. Kevin Bledsoe—released on $1,000,000 bond, pending trial for fraudulent medical activity and conspiracy to commit murder.
- Dr. William Smithson—hearing placed in abeyance pending release from medical care. Currently a patient at the inpatient unit of the York County Jail.
- Katherine Sarah Moore (aka Sarah Coleman Fortner)—previously remanded to the State Mental Facility for psychiatric evaluation and determination of fitness to stand trial.
- Jane Alma Moore (aka Danielle Morgan Herman)—remanded to the State Mental Facility for psychiatric evaluation and determination of fitness to stand trial.
- Marie Michelle Moore (aka Linda Young)—remanded to the State Mental Facility for psychiatric evaluation and determination of fitness to stand trial.

Investigation of all charges is ongoing by local, state and federal authorities. The State Medical Board is continuing its independent investigation as well.

Dr. Jack Davidson, target of several murder attempts by the group, is recuperating at home. He has been interviewed by numerous national journalists, and has been the subject of several local and national television specials. His plans for resuming his surgical career are incomplete at this time.

A further revelation in this slowly unfolding saga is the identification of Maggie M. Smithson, wife of Dr. William (Bill) Smithson, as the estranged stepmother of the Moore sisters.

The sisters had purposefully abandoned her approximately ten years earlier for her failure to intercede in their childhood abuse at the hands of their now deceased physician father. Mrs. Smithson had moved to Chapel Hill where she met and married her husband, there on sabbatical from Midsouth to attend medical school. She had not recognized the sisters due to modifying plastic surgery performed in the interim.

Chapter 36

Evansville, N.C.—Winter 2006

Jack and Lynn spent a quiet evening at home contemplating the events of the preceding months.

"You know that you're lucky to be alive", Lynn said to Jack. She continued to work on her quilt as she spoke.

"I know that now, Honey.

You know, it's really scary to be in a coma. I thought that I was dreaming ... I could see and hear what was going on around me, but I couldn't move. And no one could hear me, even though I thought I was speaking. I certainly don't ever want to repeat that experience. It was far worse than I ever could have imagined.

Doctors are used to being in control, and in that situation I had no control at all ... and it was terrifying. It was like what people describe as an out of body experience when they almost die."

"I'm just glad that you're here and safe", Lynn replied.

"But in the future, if you're asked to investigate anything by the hospital, please do it as a group project. There's safety in numbers, you know."

"Thanks for the advice. But I think I've learned my lesson. The next time ... if there is one ... in addition to group action, if I detect any criminal activity I'll certainly tell the police everything I know and let them call the shots.

You know, Hon, I'm going to be hobbling around with this cane for a while yet, but if it's all the same with you, I thought I'd go back to work next week. Jim Akins says it's ok with him, and the girls at the office have everything about ready for my return. The new office will be ready in a month or so. I'm anxious to get back."

"That's fine with me. I know how you men are ... you can't sit around too long without getting bored.

And besides, I can't get any quilting done with you here in the way."

* * * *

The following week, Jack was welcomed back to the office by his staff ... and to the hospital with a surprise party in the I.C.U. organized by Elaine and Sharon.

It had been the longest time that he had been away from clinical medicine since the day that he had started medical school almost thirty years earlier. The respite from clinical duties and call schedules had been nice, but the circumstances under which it had occurred had not been so pleasant.

Jack was en route to the hospital parking lot after picking up some papers; it was his first day "on call" for the E.R. in almost four months. He reminisced about all the times in the past he had been on call, and all the urgent problems that he had been called upon to handle. But now, he would be more than happy to settle for a quiet day.

As he was getting into his car, as if by some magical coincidence, his beeper sounded.

"Damn, it's the E.R."

He grabbed his cell phone and speed dialed the E.R. number.

The familiar voice of June, the E.R. secretary greeted him.

"Welcome back, Dr. Davidson. Please hold for Dr. Jackson. He needs to speak to you urgently about an auto accident with three badly hurt victims."

Jack got back out of his car, and hobbled toward the E.R., just opposite the parking lot.

"Another great day in the making", he thought to himself.

"God, it's great to be back!"

Epilogue

▼

Evansville, N.C.—Winter 2006

Eventually, over one hundred separate lawsuits were filed against the people involved in the cover up, as well as against Midsouth. It was the worst such case of medical fraud in the nation's history.

Numerous out of court settlements totaled into the millions of dollars. Many more lawsuits were pending action in a court system overwhelmed by the magnitude of claims filed in a single jurisdiction.

Matthew Gates not only represented Carol Smith and Tina Rouse, but countless others as well. As a result, he had become quite famous ... as well as wealthy and was being considered a possible gubernatorial candidate by the state Republican Party.

Bill Smithson, Jr. had been only too happy to return to his practice in Raleigh and fade into anonymity; the Smithson name had been smeared enough thanks to his father's actions.

And for their parts in the fraud and attempted murder of Jack Davidson, the following dispositions were eventually made:

- Kevin Bledsoe, M.D.—sentenced to five to fifteen years in the state penitentiary.

- Russell Callahan, M.D.—sentenced to fifteen to twenty-five years in the state penitentiary, minimum ten years prior to parole consideration.

- David Fortner, M.D.—sentenced to five to fifteen years in the state penitentiary; for his help in concluding the group's actions, a plea for time reduction was being considered.

- Carl Hauser, M.D.—sentenced to five to fifteen years in the state penitentiary.
- Michael Herman, M.D.—sentenced to five to fifteen years in the state penitentiary.
- Frank Li, M.D.—sentenced to five to fifteen years in the state penitentiary.
- William Smithson, M.D.—sentenced to five to fifteen years in the state penitentiary.
- The Moore sisters: Katie, Jane and Marie—continued undergoing psychiatric evaluation and treatment at the state mental facility. The severity of their problem would probably preclude any prison time.

Appeals are ongoing.

Maggie Smithson was found dead at her home approximately six months following the tragedy that had taken her husband to prison and placed her stepdaughters in the state psychiatric hospital.

A suicide note indicated that she had been depressed due to the separation from her husband and the rejection she had received from the Moore sisters.

Cindy Li filed for divorce from her husband six months after moving back to her home in New Hampshire.

Jennifer Bledsoe returned home to Oregon, vowing to continue aiding her husband's appeal of his sentence, and maintaining her devotion to him. However, seven months later, she filed for divorce. She married her tennis instructor at the local country club the day after the divorce was finalized.

Matters related to health care delivery and remuneration for services rendered by physicians continue to deteriorate despite attempts by physicians to organize and unite against the insurance industry and the federal government.

The powerful insurance lobby, backed by the unlimited funding of the industry it represents, will undoubtedly continue to plague the medical profession until such time that the American public finally challenges their right to control premiums and payments. The American public demands ... and deserves ... the best medical care that the world has to offer. But they need to let their insurance carriers know that physicians and hospitals rendering that care have a right to a just and timely payment.

Meanwhile, prospects for the future of the medical profession continue to deteriorate, as evidenced by both decreasing applications to medical schools, and the decreased academic quality of those applicants. Medical malpractice claims continue to spiral upward, fueled by a lack of laws limiting claim awards. Medical malpractice insurance premiums continue to rise as a result, further limiting physician's incomes and further diminishing the attractiveness of the once most sought after and admired profession.

After his near death experience, Dr. Jack Davidson, while actively engaged in the practice of surgery, is considering a career change and is exploring business opportunities.

End

About the Author

John Richard Langley a.k.a. Jack Langley, M.D. was born in Meriden, Connecticut. Raised in a military family, he has lived in numerous parts of the country as well as Guam and Hawaii.

He was educated at The University of South Carolina, Columbia, S.C. (A.B. English) and the Medical University of South Carolina, Charleston, S.C. (M.D.). Following general surgery residency (Eastern Virginia Medical School, Norfolk, Virginia) and vascular surgery fellowship (University of Kansas Medical Center, Kansas City, Kansas) he entered private practice in North Carolina.

He now resides in Cumming, Georgia, operates Greater Atlanta Vein Clinic, P.C. in Alpharetta, Georgia and does Locum Tenens surgery, with assignments ranging from Maine to Alaska. He is currently licensed in twelve states.

He is married to the former Janet Schmidt of Oconto Falls, Wisconsin. They have three children: Maria, of Flowery Branch, Georgia; John Rudolph (Rudy) of Greensboro, North Carolina and Tiffany of Canton, Georgia.

His hobbies include fiction writing, poetry, photography and travel.

He is the author of ***Murder at Charing Cross***, previously published by iUniverse Press (2006).

978-0-595-42371-2
0-595-42371-X

Printed in the United States
70682LV00005B/28-42